Gaia's legs were in motion before he saw anything coming. This was a tactic she'd learned from some of the darker passages of the *Go Rin No Sho*, the ancient book of martial arts philosophy her dad had forced her to read all those years ago. It was a cheap shot, at least by the standards of honorable combat—by holding her enemy's gaze, she'd drawn his attention away from the impending kick. Even as she leaped into the air, her limbs a whirl of focused power, she kept staring at him . . . staring and staring until *crack!*—her left foot connected with his temple.

He collapsed to the ground.

"No!" the othergirl shrieked.

Stunned, Gaia regained her balance. The girl fell at the guy's side. She slapped his pale cheeks, frantically trying to revive him, then shot Gaia a furious glare.

"What did you do *that* for?" she barked.

"I, uh—I thought. . . ." Gaia had no idea what to say.

Something was very wrong here.

Don't miss any books in this thrilling new series
from Pocket Books:

FEARLESS™

All Pocket Book titles are available by post from:
Simon & Schuster Cash Sales, P.O. Box 29,
Douglas, Isle of Man IM99 1BQ
Credit cards accepted. Please telephone 01624 836000,
Fax 01624 670923, Internet http://www.bookpost.co.uk
or email: bookshop@enterprise.net for details

FEARLESS

FRANCINE PASCAL

FLEE

POCKET
BOOKS

An imprint of Simon & Schuster UK Ltd
A Viacom Company
Africa House, 64-78 Kingsway, London WC2B 6AH

Produced by 17th Street Productions, Inc.
33 West 17th Street, New York, NY 10011

A CIP catalogue record for this book is
available from the British Library

ISBN 07434 15396

1 3 5 7 9 10 8 6 4 2

Printed and bound in Great Britain by Omnia Books Ltd, Glasgow

I'm considering giving up
chess. As in never playing again.
Not even in Washington Square Park
with Mr. Haq or Zolov or Renny.
Definitely not with Sam. Not with
anybody. The fact of the matter is
that I *can't* play anymore. I've
lost my edge. The game confuses
me. The last few times I played, I
couldn't strategize. I was losing
left and right. And for a grand
master, that's humiliating.

More to the point, my life has
always felt like chess, like combat. Life makes its move, and I
make mine. Maybe I haven't been
exactly comfortable with the
setup, but at the very least I've
been used to it. It's all I've
ever really known.

Now it seems like I'm no
longer even a player in my own
game. I feel more like a pawn.
And I'm not even sure of the
sides. In the past it was easy to
make out black from white, but
now the board is a blur of gray.

Who is the white knight? My

father or my Uncle Oliver?

I've had my doubts about all
of this before. But I've never
been as confused as I am now. The
simple facts are these: my father
is gone again, and Oliver is
back—asking me to live with him.
And Sam? I can't even go there.
My feelings about him are a negative image of what they once
were: where I once had something
pure and instinctive and a hundred percent right, I now have
only empty, bitter pain.

Yesterday I tried to think of
one constant in my life.
Instinctively, of course, I
turned to my friendship with Ed.
But I nixed the thought before it
even made it to the surface. Ed
is a new person. There's no denying that I feel strange around
him. I can't put my finger on
exactly what has changed between
us, but now that he's up and
walking, there's a self-conscious
awkwardness between us that I've
never felt before.

Which of course makes me wonder if Ed isn't the one who has
changed.

Maybe it's me.

And all of this thinking just
sends me further into a spiral of
uncertainty. I don't have time
for it. I need to make some cold,
hard decisions. To live with
Oliver or not? God. What I would
give for some advice right now.
I've never much been one for taking (or asking for) advice, but
I'm fresh out of strategies. The
chessboard is a blank slate. A
tabla rasa, as they used to say
in ancient Rome. I'm unable to
think for myself at all.

Sometimes I feel like confid-
ing in Mrs. Moss, and I find
myself almost bursting out and
telling her or Paul everything,
my whole story—complete with all
of the shit and misery and loneliness. But then I remember
myself. Living with the Moss
family is a temporary arrangement. I'm not going to sleep in

Mary's room forever, no matter how hospitable her family is. Besides, these are good people. They don't need to be burdened with my problems.

Anyway, they can't help me.

No one can help me figure out if Oliver is just screwing with my head, or if he's really the well-meaning uncle he claims to be. So I have to rely on my own judgment. And that's a shame, since it migrated south for the winter a long time ago. So what do I do? Run to Oliver or away from him? Believe what he says—that my father is actually "Loki" and has been brainwashing me? Or do I tell Oliver to drop dead?

I have to go back to the facts, though. I have to ignore my emotion. After all, emotion clouds reason. That's one of the first lessons of martial arts. And the facts are indisputable. Oliver has come for me twice, while my father has abandoned me twice. *He's* here now. My father

isn't. That should count for
something. . . right?

I'm not a girl who hesitates.
I make my move and accept the
consequences. So I should do it.
Leave the Mosses and give Oliver
another chance to prove himself.
I mean, if I don't go, how will I
know?

It makes the most sense.

So why am I hesitating?

Car accident,
mugging, hit,
whatever. The
means didn't
matter, only **the**
the end: Josh
unexpected
lying in a
pool of
blood.

"THAT'S THE LONGEST SUBWAY RIDE

Cheap Joke

I've ever taken," Ed Fargo groaned as he and Gaia emerged from the dark stairwell and into the bright sunshine. "What's with the sudden interest in Harlem?"

Gaia smirked. "This isn't Harlem, Ed."

"Whatever." He repositioned himself on his crutches, squinting for a moment at the bright blue sky—then he glanced up the winding street toward a shady little park, where the leaves were just starting to bud on the trees. "It's the boondocks."

That's why I came, Gaia answered silently. *Because nothing that's familiar feels right.* So here they were, at the Cloisters: an old monastery-turned-museum that looked like a medieval fortress, perched over the Hudson River—way up at the top of Manhattan, in Washington Heights. If you lived in Greenwich Village, this was the middle of nowhere.

Gaia was thinking that maybe a change of scene would help her see her life below Fourteenth Street more clearly. Downtown, it was a landscape of confusion. Up here, maybe she'd get some perspective. She'd sort out her feelings about Oliver. Her father. Sam. She stole a sideways glance at Ed, then added him to that list.

Maybe I should have come alone.

Ed hobbled forward, swinging his legs between his crutches, limping with surprising precision. Gaia followed silently by his side as they entered the park. Normally she didn't mind long silences with Ed. In fact, a lot of times she preferred them to his barrage of one-liners. But today she craved conversation. Yet still she didn't say one word, not even when they stopped for a lemonade slushie. She couldn't even be cheered by the extra-sweet fake-lemon syrup flowing into her cup. It was a good scene: a Slurpee, Ed, sunlight dappling the almost bare branches of the park, the rough stone walls of the Cloisters looming ahead of them. . . a perfectly excellent day, by any standards.

But the knot in Gaia's stomach didn't loosen, and she doubted it would anytime soon.

"Are there any monks here?" Ed asked, licking the syrupy ice and glancing at the imposing structure. His voice was light, but his dark brown eyes were searching. *He knows something's up with me,* Gaia thought, shrugging by way of answer. Of course he knew something was up with her. He was Ed, for God's sake. And usually, when she was pissed at the world, she couldn't wait to spill to him, to get his take. She stared into space, feeling his curious eyes on her. She *was* desperate to share all the turmoil whirling like laundry in an endless spin cycle inside her brain. But somehow. . . she couldn't.

Something stood between them now. Some new gap. Some new. . . *what?* What was so different about him? Sure, he could walk. But he was still the same dry, no-bullshit Ed he'd always been.

Maybe.

Gaia averted her eyes from his gaze. She knew that this new eye-to-eye, face-to-face dynamic was part of the problem. It would just take some getting used to. That was all. Or maybe not. Maybe everything would deteriorate. Why should her friendship with Ed survive all of its rocky patches when every other relationship of hers had bitten the proverbial dust?

". . . every bit as bad as rats, but somehow humans detest rats more," Ed was suddenly babbling away, pointing at a squirrel hovering over a garbage bin. Clearly he didn't enjoy the silence, either. Gaia nodded every few seconds like a marionette, floating off on a sea of self-pity. *Pathetic,* she chided herself. But feelings were feelings. There was no way to stop them from surfacing, from coming out of nowhere to smack you on the head and leave you dizzy.

Or. . . maybe the real problem was hope. Like believing you could take some time out to get perspective when your name was Gaia Moore. Like hoping you could enjoy yourself, even for an afternoon. . . .

She swallowed hard. All at once she could feel one of those extremely annoying sobbing fits welling up inside her. With every ounce of her strength, she fought it back. She didn't want to lose it here, now, with Ed. Hope: that was the problem. Hope was a cheap joke without a punch line. Gaia jump-cut her way through a series of images from the past six months, culminating with her father's disappearance. A lot of reason for hope there, right? It was almost funny.

Except that it's my life.

". . . what's going on in G-land?" Ed was asking.

"Huh?" She jerked, then stared down at her sneakers, blushing. It was a first, she realized. She'd never blushed around Ed before. What the hell was her problem? Why did a goddamned wheelchair—or lack of one—mean so much?

Ed just laughed mildly. "You haven't exactly been your most verbal self today."

Gaia shrugged. "Yeah, well," she muttered. "I guess what with everything. . . you know, my father. He took off again. I told you all this."

Ed's laughter died. "Have you heard from him?"

"Nope." She took a slug of her slushie and held the ice chips in her mouth for a moment, in some attempt to freeze out the unwanted thoughts, to freeze out doubt, second guessing, endless questions. But it didn't work. "I haven't. And everything—" She paused, her voice catching as if on some invisible shard of glass. She couldn't go on. And now she was *truly* embarrassed, tears rising in her throat. Christ. *What is wrong with me?*

"Come on," Ed murmured. His voice was soothing. He gestured toward a patch of grass under an old oak tree.

Gaia followed him silently.

He balanced the crutches against the tree, then eased himself down to the ground, lying on his side and propping his head up on his elbow. Gaia sat cross-legged—facing him but not meeting his thoughtful stare. She picked at the blades of grass.

"Do you want to talk about it?" he asked tentatively.

This should be Sam.

The thought came from nowhere, slicing through Gaia's brain like a bullet. But she couldn't deny it. Sam was the one who should be there with her on the grass, helping her figure out what to do about Oliver, helping her sort through the mess that her life had become. And that was the real tragedy: it wasn't Sam, and it never would be Sam. The Sam Moon chapter of her life had closed. Forever. She had to accept it and move on.

"I'm. . . confused," Gaia admitted at long last, opting at least to speak. "I can't tell my ass from my elbow."

"One's sharp and pointy," Ed joked.

Gaia mustered a smile. She turned a blade of grass in her fingers. Details of Sam assembled themselves in her mind: his sandy brown curls, his amber gold eyes, the freckles that dotted his shoulder blades. Her chest tightened. Suddenly being with Ed felt inexplicably uncomfortable again. She shifted her gaze over to the Cloister buildings, to a large stone cross adorning a sloping slate roof.

"How anyone can believe in God is beyond me," she muttered, almost to herself. "Everything is random."

"Yeah," Ed agreed, rolling onto his back and staring up at the deep blue sky. "I'm down with the existential thinking myself. It's all random. But you know, G, that means there's just as much random good as there is random shit. Take my accident, for example. That was a random awful thing. Then take my walking again. That was random luck. Random experimental science."

Gaia forced another smile, then drained the rest of her Slurpee and placed the cup beside her. For a moment, she closed her eyes. The cool breeze felt nice against her face. She wished she could stay like that for a year. Not thinking, not talking, not interacting. Just *being*.

"No matter how bad it gets, remember: random luck can come your way," Ed said. "The odds are just as good."

Maybe that was true. Gaia cracked open one eye. Sure, Ed's words did make some sense. But where did it leave her? No closer to sorting the random good from the random bad, the wheat from the chaff, the Olivers from the Toms.

"My uncle wants me to go live with him," Gaia heard herself say.

"He *what?*" Ed shot up on his elbow, his eyes widening. "The guy's supposed to be in some loony-bin supermax prison. Right?"

Gaia bit her lip. "He escaped. He has his own version about what's what." She took a deep breath, and before she knew it, the entire story was pouring out of her: the note her father left, Oliver's bizarre appearance at the Mosses', the loneliness, the confusion, the betrayal... and as the words flowed, she felt the smallest hint of relief, from somewhere deep inside. Just a touch. Ed had a quick mind. He didn't ask stupid questions. He simply followed the story, examined the scenario analytically, then gave his opinion.

"I think you should stay with the Mosses for a while," he said.

Gaia nodded. It was the simplest answer and probably the best. But then, Ed didn't know what it was like not to have a family. He didn't know what it was like to live with someone else's parents. To always wish for your own.

"He could easily be playing you," Ed said forcefully. "It's too dangerous to go live with him."

"But what if he's telling the truth?" Gaia mumbled, her eyes dropping back to the ground.

Ed sighed. "This is a tough one. We're talking probabilities here. It's all hypothetical."

"So where does that leave me? Back at square one."

"Which is why you should stay with the Mosses," Ed retorted. "You *are* absolutely sure of them. You're *not* absolutely sure of your uncle. Or your dad. Or anyone. But you do know you're safe with the Mosses, that no one there has any agenda."

She looked up into his eyes. "But I can't stay with them forever," she whispered.

"So stay until you're more sure of which way to go. After all, if Oliver really is the good guy he says he is, he won't be going anywhere soon. So he can wait."

Gaia shot Ed a grateful smile. What was it about him? He could always find a way to untangle things, to take a pile of jumbled, ratty strands and pull them apart. He smiled back, and suddenly she became aware of how close together they were lying—his elbow almost touching hers, which was a weird thought because she was quite sure their elbows had touched before. . . and so what, anyway? But for some reason it was different now—*Stop*. She didn't like the way her thoughts were going at all. She had enough drama in her life. She didn't need to be making something out of nothing. "Let's go see if there are any monks in there," she said, standing up abruptly.

"HOW MUCH?" SAM ASKED, POINTING

Daydreaming

at a bucket that was filled with big bunches of pink lilies wrapped in cellophane.

"Ten dollars," the shopkeeper answered curtly.

Sam picked out a crumpled ten from his wallet, handed it to the man, and grabbed one of the bunches. It was only as he stepped away from the deli that he felt like a true idiot. Flowers. From a deli, no less. Such a cheap form of truce. *Nothing says "sorry" quite like pink flowers!* Sam shook his head and squeezed his eyes shut. This kind of cliché had no place in his relationship with Gaia. It had nothing to do with them.

But words hadn't worked. So what else was there? Maybe just the rituals left to the thousands of other couples who struggled to keep their shit together: flowers, make-up dinners. . . couples therapy. Sam snorted at that one. But the thought alone was enough to dampen his mood even more. Buying flowers for Gaia was lame. Period.

How do you know? Sam's inner voice countered as he waited for the light on Columbus Avenue to change. True, he couldn't say anything for sure when it came to Gaia these days. She had closed herself off to him, as he had done to her. They were strangers now. Which was why a gesture—any gesture—had to be made. Before it was too late.

15

Sam hurried down West Eighty-third Street toward Central Park West, tightening his grip on the dripping flowers. As he neared the Mosses' opulent apartment building, he wiped a hand across his chapped lips and wished for the millionth time that week that Josh Kendall would die. Car accident, mugging, hit, whatever. The means didn't matter, only the end: Josh lying in a pool of blood. Out of Sam's life once and for all.

But even if Sam had it in him—even if he were another person, capable of murder and not himself— he knew the story wouldn't end there; Josh was just a link in the chain. The directives, the threats on Gaia's life, the orders to ferry packages from place to place. . . all of it filtered through Josh from some other source, one who kept well out of the way, deep in the shadows.

Them, as Sam liked to say in his private thoughts.

What could he say to Gaia as he handed her these flowers? He could never communicate to her that everything he did was out of love—including all of his silences, all of his disappearances, all of his night- mares. . . because Josh had made it very clear that Gaia would be harmed if one microscopic speck of information passed from Sam's lips to her. A small, bitter smile tweaked the corner of Sam's mouth as he considered his boldest moments, when he'd truly thought he could walk away from all of this with maybe just a black eye from Josh as punishment.

So much for daydreaming.

Sam hesitated on the corner, eyeing the awning. The uniformed doorman was lurking outside the glass doors. It was a different guy from the other night, though—this one was older, shorter, and fatter. Good. The doorman from the other night probably thought Sam was nuts. He wouldn't be too far off the mark, either. Apparently love brought out crazy sides of a person. And losing love? That prospect could turn a guy psycho.

Still. . . this new doorman did pose an obstacle, because he would have to buzz up to Gaia to let her know that Sam was here. And she probably wouldn't let him in. And what if somebody else answered? Someone like—

Brendan.

Sam stiffened.

Well, well. Think of the devil. Brendan Moss marched out the doors, nodded politely to the doorman, then paused on the sidewalk to zip up his windbreaker. Sam felt a familiar expanding hollowness. He knew this sensation well. It came to him all the time now: despair. He also knew he should try to get the hell out of there before Brendan saw him, but his legs seemed to have frozen solid. . . .

Too late.

As Brendan glanced down the avenue in Sam's direction, his stout features hardened. He immediately strode toward Sam, his footsteps falling like bricks. "What the hell are you doing here?" he barked.

Sam blinked. "I'm here to see Gaia," he said softly.

Brendan's face was a mask of stone. He shot a hard stare at the flowers.

Was it only a matter of months since Brendan had stopped being his friend? Looking at him now, his face a smear of hatred, Sam felt like years had passed since they'd shared suite B4 in the NYU dorm. And evidently Brendan felt like it had been only minutes since they'd had their fistfight. Jesus. Sam still found it hard to believe that he could have so much anger inside himself, such an ugly streak. It seemed surreal. Still. That had nothing to do with seeing Gaia. *And God knows,* Sam thought, looking at Brendan's coldly glittering eyes, *he wasn't exactly a loyal friend to me. . .* Okay, maybe Brendan hadn't deserved all of the rage he'd gotten. But he'd deserved a good chunk of it, yes.

"Get the hell out of here," Brendan spat.

Now this. Did it all have to be so hard, so complicated? Couldn't Brendan just step back for once? Drop the hatred? Cut Sam one tiny bit of slack? "Brendan, man," Sam said . "Please. Gaia and I have stuff to talk about. We—"

"I haven't forgotten what you did to Mike," Brendan interrupted in a low, harsh voice. "If you think I'm letting a killer near Gaia, you're sadly mistaken."

He thinks I'm a killer.

Sam Moon shook his head. There was no point in trying to pursue this conversation. Without another word, he turned and headed back across West Eighty-third, to the opposite corner. There was a garbage can there. He dropped the flowers on top of a half-eaten sandwich and a newspaper, shoved his hands into his pockets, and walked south. Maybe Brendan had done him a favor. After all, it was better to have Brendan Moss tell him to get lost than Gaia.

What a piece of luck.

TOM MOORE SHIVERED IN THE CHILL

Pale Blue Eyes

of the morning. Brussels. Not his favorite European city. It was elegant, but cold and impersonal—with a threat of rain always hanging in the gray northern light.

"Encore de café, monsieur?" the waitress asked pleasantly as she approached his table at the brasserie.

"Oui, merci." Tom smiled at her as she refilled his coffee cup. Her forehead was creased in puzzlement. Evidently she thought he was a little strange, sitting

outside on such a damp, miserable day. But Tom had to stay put, despite the far more alluring warmth and light emanating from behind the glass door. He had an assignment. This was the agreed-upon spot: outdoors at Café Belgique, on the corner of Brussels' main square, Grand Place. Tom checked his watch again, then gave the square a quick once-over, scanning both for his contact and for anyone who might not belong: a particularly obvious tourist, a sweet-faced woman in her twenties. These were the people who could put a bullet through his heart. Expect the unexpected. It was the only way to stay alive.

But the square was empty. A drizzle had started.

Tom swallowed, pulling his hat over his ears. He shouldn't be here. He should be in New York, with Gaia, protecting her. But he had to put her out of his mind—at least until he had a clear picture of what Loki was trying to accomplish, and more important, where he was. At this point he simply had to stay alive as long as possible. The best way to do so was to obey the Agency's wishes. Self-preservation was his second-highest priority. Right after Gaia.

Expect the unexpected, he repeated to himself, and a wave of frustration overcame him. He'd failed to do exactly that. He'd gotten sloppy. He'd assumed that Loki wouldn't use any decoys or traps, that his intention would be clear. But once again Tom had underestimated his brother's cleverness. He shouldn't have done so—not when his last informant vanished before his eyes at that Berlin train station. Tracking Tom to Brussels would only be a matter of time. The circle was closing in.

Tom forced down another mouthful of scalding coffee. The caffeine sent a queasy rush through his veins. He was bone weary after days of scampering from Berlin to Frankfurt to Brussels, dodging what he felt instinctively were watching eyes. His stubbly jaw tightened. Emotional blackmail. That's precisely what this was. If Tom weren't so used to the manipulations of both the Agency and his brother, the anger might have consumed him. But instead he let it drive him. Which was exactly what the Agency counted on.

He sighed as he sucked down the dregs of his cup, then glanced down at his watch. 0800 on the nail. His contact should arrive imminently: Henrik van de Meulen, an Interpol agent whom the Agency had contacted on Tom's behalf after the Berlin incident. A man with connections . . .

Sure enough, he heard light footsteps approaching from the rear. He turned in his chair and found himself looking up into the pale blue eyes of a tall man with graying blond hair, bundled in an overcoat.

"Good morning," the man stated. His voice was clipped and heavily accented. "Henrik van de Meulen."

Tom shook his hand. He had never met Henrik, but his face was instantly familiar from many photographs.

The man had history with George Niven, and George had spoken highly of his intelligence and professionalism—both of which seemed to come through in his half smile and clear, alert expression. George was frugal with praise.

"I am very pleased to meet you at last," Henrik said as he seated himself. "George has always spoken well of you. I'm only sorry the circumstances under which we are meeting could not be more. . . pleasant."

Tom nodded. His throat felt dry and flinty, as if he'd been breathing in a coal mine. An image of Gaia flashed in front of him, her gold blond hair not unlike the color of Henrik's. The informant in Berlin had said her name just before Loki's men had got to him. *Gaia. . . kidnapping . . .*

"Do you have anything for me?" Tom asked, low and urgent.

Henrik turned nonchalantly, as if looking for the waitress, but Tom knew that movement, too: it was knitted into his very bones. That slight shift of gaze. Henrik was in fact surreptitiously checking the square and the double doors of the brasserie. "I think so," he murmured. "But before we do this, tell me, how is your daughter?" He trained concerned eyes on Tom. "Is she safe?"

Safe. The word sounded odd, foreign—even though keeping Gaia safe was the one goal Tom knew intimately, the only thing he cared about, the sole reason behind everything he did. Safe. Yet at that moment it sounded not like a state of being but more like a place. Some mythical land that Tom did not and could not know, an inaccessible fairy-tale island not found on any map. . . .

"I don't know," Tom replied truthfully, wishing the question had never been asked at all, wondering if he would ever be able to answer that question in the affirmative. "The Agency is keeping tabs. . . and George is taking care of her, but—"

"Then you need not worry," Henrik interjected swiftly. "You are leaving your daughter in George's very capable hands."

"Yes."

Tom smiled thinly at Henrik; he could draw little comfort from the words. True, George Niven was a trusted friend—perhaps Tom's only true friend in the world. But Loki was a true enemy.

"I have a daughter, too." Henrik smiled and signaled to the waitress to bring him coffee. "Can I see a picture of Gaia?"

Tom fumbled for his wallet, retrieving the photo he'd been carrying with him since their trip to Paris. Again his throat tightened. In Paris he and Gaia had forged a new relationship after all that separation. They'd reconnected as father and daughter—only to have that bond severed. The image brought a fresh surge of pain: Gaia smiling in a hooded sweatshirt, standing outside Notre Dame in the rain, her incredible hair snaking down her shoulders, completely soaked.

"She hates having her picture taken," he muttered, trying to smile.

"Yes," Henrik remarked admiringly. "I can see the fearlessness of which George has spoken. It is here." He tapped the picture. "In her eyes."

Tom quickly shoved the photograph back into his wallet. He couldn't look at it anymore. Gaia's fearlessness didn't make him worry less about her. God, it was a curse, not a blessing. Fear was an instinct designed to keep a species alive. Without it, Gaia was fair game. For Loki.

"Let's get to it," Tom muttered. "What do you have?"

To: L
From: S
Date: March 4
File: 002
Subject: Enigma
   Awaiting instructions.

To: S
From: L
Date: March 4
File: 002
Subject: Enigma
   Enigma to be taken alive at all costs.
Exercise extreme caution.

There is nothing worse than being almost home, stuck in traffic, in a holding pattern. You can see your prize, but you can't touch it.

Recently I've been thinking about all the speeches I have been forced to make to Gaia—all the lies or embellished truths. I've been ruminating over the meaninglessness and intangibility of words. What are they? They are nothing; they are made of air, made of whatever I have at my disposal so as to nudge Gaia toward enlightenment. But soon she will see. She will see that I am the only person who knows how to shape her life. The only one capable of nurturing all her magnificent potential.

Once again I have planted the seed of a fledgling trust between us. She has cracked the door ajar and allowed me to speak through it. This is a highly significant development. She could have slammed it in my face. And I must

do nothing to jeopardize our
fragile new bond. I must let her
sort through her conflicting
feelings, alone. She is suspi-
cious, hostile—and rightly so.
She has been told to hate me. But
I sense her vacillation.

An encounter with Gaia is like
an encounter with a wild animal:
she is vulnerable, untamed, cir-
cumspect, all instincts on alert.
There is only one way to win such
an animal over. Let the animal
know you are there—but do not
step toward it, or it will run.

Let it know it can trust you
by doing absolutely nothing.
Nothing at all.

And this is the worst part:
the tense wait. She has not
sent word. She has not said a
thing since I entreated her to
come abroad with me. But though
Gaia is skeptical of my own
good faith, I trust her implic-
itly. I trust she knows what is
good for her, *who* is good for
her. And when the full glory of

.

her destiny is finally revealed
to her, she will not only meet
it, but embrace it.

   And if she doesn't?

   Oh, but she will.

   One way or the other, she
will.

A man in
pain,
looking for
an answer.   **DNA**
Or maybe he
was just a
man going
mad.

SAM KNEW SHE'D BE IN THE PARK.

Somehow, even at this late hour, even though she'd moved uptown to live with the Mosses, he knew she'd be right here—alone under the miniature Arc de Triomphe, searching for whatever it was she'd always searched for in the middle of the night.

That counted for something, didn't it? That he could still anticipate her moves?

Maybe. Or maybe not. He swallowed. The motives behind those moves were still as mysterious as they were that first day he'd spotted her here.

Gaia, he wanted to say. But he couldn't open his mouth. He could only watch her.

It was incredible. Normally the pale lamplight of Washington Square Park made a person look sickly or tired. Not her. In a way, she was even more breathtaking here than she was in the sun. But maybe the force of his reaction just had to do with his longing for her, his *starvation* for her. He drank in her outfit: the moss-green hooded sweatshirt with frayed edges, a pair of ancient jeans with a rip near her thigh—

"Sam?"

He jerked. He hadn't even noticed she had seen him. But she was staring at him, her eyes wide with... what? Anger, perhaps. Disgust, more likely.

"Gaia," he said. His voice rang with much more strength than he felt. "I just. . . I have to say one thing to you."

She stood there. Her face registered no response. But what did he expect? That she should say something encouraging, like, "Great, go ahead"? On the other hand, she didn't bolt or curse him out, either. Maybe that counted for something, too. Gaia shot him the ghost of a smile. Or maybe he'd just imagined it. But for moment she looked like the old Gaia, the girl whose toughness and defiance was just a shield for pain. That shield was something they both had in common. Sam could still try. Now was the moment to reach out to her; he could feel her openness, see a shred of something like love still glinting in her eyes.

And then the look was gone.

Too late. Sam's throat constricted.

"What do you want?" Gaia asked.

"I miss you," he found himself choking out. "I can't do this anymore. You're all I think about." His voice broke. "This is too hard. I mean, I know I've always had a hard time saying exactly what's on my mind—"

"That's an understatement," Gaia spat. "And you know what? You're still not saying what's on your mind. You want to know something? You're a smart guy. But right now you sound like you're reciting lines from a bad soap opera. Stop talking around things. Say what you want to say or leave me alone."

Sam blinked. For a moment he almost felt angry. The cold, impersonal words she'd barked at him were like a kick from behind, one that smarts and sends a twinge of rage through the body. They were almost insulting. He wasn't some anonymous "smart guy." He was *Sam*. Sam Moon. Her goddamned boyfriend. Or ex-boyfriend. Or whatever. And who was *she* to tell him not to talk around things?

But as soon as the anger came upon him, it subsided. He had no right to be angry at her. None at all. He'd tormented her relentlessly. Yes, he'd done that to protect her, but there was no denying that he'd destroyed their relationship. He'd *dumped* her. He'd left her in the park, alone with Brendan's brother, because he knew that if he hung around any longer, he'd get them both shot to death.

Some relationship.

"I'm waiting," Gaia stated.

"I don't want us to be apart anymore," Sam breathed. His voice was low, urgent. "I was wrong. I've *been* wrong. I have to be with you. That's all that matters."

He took a step forward.

Gaia took a step back.

This was torture. No, this was bullshit. It had to stop. "Please, Gaia, let me tell you what's going on." Uttering that sentence was like pushing a boulder up a hill. "I'm ready—"

"Doesn't this feel like déjà vu?" Gaia interrupted, her voice flat.

Sam's eyes narrowed. The night suddenly seemed very cold and dark. "What do you mean?"

"We've already had this conversation," she said. Her eyes flashed around the park once more, almost as if she was expecting somebody to appear out of the shadows. "A dozen times. It's boring. It doesn't serve any purpose."

"But I. . . ." Sam closed his mouth. It was ironic, wasn't it? The last time he'd seen her—that day in the park—she'd asked him: *"Who are you, Sam? I don't even know."* And now he was feeling that exact same emotion toward her. She was wearing more than the usual protective shield. `This furtive android was not Gaia Moore.` Something else was going on—something besides the decimation of their relationship. This girl was a stranger.

"What's going on, Gaia?" he whispered.

"Why don't you tell me?" she shot back. "I can't deal with you, Sam. I can't deal with whatever secret life you have. I've suffered plenty because of other people's secrets. I'm through with that."

She was talking about her father, of course—and once again Sam felt anger stirring inside him. Lumping Sam with that man was grossly unfair. The circumstances were completely different. Tom Moore seemed to relish his life of intrigue and deception. He was willing to abandon his daughter at a moment's notice for secrets and lies and danger. Sam, on the other hand, had been forced into it—blackmailed into a nightmare he couldn't control. *Tell her!* It was on the tip of his tongue. Let Josh come and get him. At least he could die knowing he'd come clean with Gaia—

"Maybe one day we can be friends again," Gaia said.

"Friends?" Sam asked, incredulous. Anger turned to rage. "Now who sounds like a soap opera? Gaia, come on. You and I can *never* be just friends. No matter—"

"Stop it." The toneless voice was back. "I've got too much on my mind."

"Too much on your mind," Sam echoed.

The energy drained from his body. His shoulders sagged. The full implication of Gaia's words settled over him. This was a frivolous exercise. It would accomplish nothing. And he knew that he would never tell her the truth because he would never allow himself to put her life in jeopardy. Besides, it was very clear she didn't even know how to act around him anymore. She was keeping a secret from him, too—and she had no intention of sharing it. Not with Sam Moon, anyway. He was no longer a priority for her. He was on the back burner. He'd put himself there by living a lie. And when all was said and done, it came down to this: Sam loved Gaia too much to save their relationship. He'd chosen to save her life instead. And he always would, until one of them ended up dead. End of story.

"Later, Sam," she said quietly. She turned and hurried under the Arc de Triomphe, vanishing down Waverly Place into the night.

"Yeah," Sam replied to the empty park. "Later."

Something occurred to him at that moment. Josh and his cohorts must have foreseen that this would happen. They'd used his love for Gaia against him, corrupting the one sacred relationship he had in this world. They'd made it very clear from the start that Sam had to stay away from Gaia—and when he wouldn't, they'd driven a wedge between him and Gaia with lies and fear. Their breaking up was the inevitable result. . . which meant that once again, in the twisted game of chess that his life had become, he had been outplayed. He'd already lost.

"THE LEADS ON LOKI RAN COLD, AS

Bird
Droppings

you know," Henrik was explaining. "But we've managed to trace another—" He stopped, shifted slightly in his chair. His gaze fluttered over Tom's shoulder just for an instant. "Another potential leak," he finished.

Tom didn't bat an eyelash. He got the message, though. The body language was subtle but unequivocal. Henrik had observed some potential danger lurking nearby.

"Shall we?" Henrik said smoothly. He placed a few Belgian francs on the café table.

"Yes," Tom said.

They stood up and moved purposefully but without hurry into the brasserie. Inside, it was smoky and warm, saturated with the delicious scent of espresso. None of the customers paid any attention to them—which meant nothing, of course. For all Tom knew, every single one of them could have been employed by Loki.

"Follow me," Henrik instructed, making for a back room.

They strolled down a narrow corridor—and then suddenly they were out on a small cobbled street, striding away from the main square. "Through here," Henrik directed. They approached an alley running parallel to a used bookstore.

Tom used the back window of a parked car as a mirror to check behind them. There were no tails, at least none visible.

"Your Agency thought they were close," Henrik continued as they walked through a maze of small streets, past flower shops and chocolatiers. "But Loki was too clever for them."

"Surprise, surprise," Tom commented darkly.

Henrik nodded, shoving his hands into his overcoat pockets. "He deleted his tracks, rerouted his accounts and contacts." He shot Tom a wry smile that he didn't return. "He is, as they say in English, laughing his way to the bank."

"That's not funny," Tom muttered. Instantly he regretted the brusqueness and impatience in his tone—but the familiar hard burn of frustration was gathering inside him. Loki was always one step ahead of him. Always. Which was why Tom didn't feel he had the time to make light of his twin's profiting from death and destruction.

"Now, strictly speaking, Interpol can't help you," Henrik continued. "On the record, we have no information regarding Loki's whereabouts, his finances, or his contacts—"

"Can we just dispense with the red tape?" Tom broke in. He picked up his pace as they approached a district that he vaguely, half consciously recognized as the Sablon: mostly antique shops abutting Gothic churches. "I'm sorry, but the clock is ticking." He lowered his voice. "I don't care if it's on the record or off. You said you had something for me. It's Interpol's duty to assist me in this matter."

"Theoretically, yes on both fronts, Tom," Henrik

replied, adopting that tone of strained decorum common to diplomacy. "We do have information. Your Agency lost the thread once Loki changed course, but we think we've tracked his rerouting to a Swiss bank. Now, you're well aware that Interpol doesn't usually get involved with the Swiss. At least not openly. Such a thing can take months, even with an international security risk case as prominent as Loki's." Henrik paused to direct Tom down a narrow lane lined with junk shops. "*Especially* with one as prominent as Loki's."

A minute later they emerged into a tiny park, overgrown and ill kept. It was also empty and private. Henrik led Tom through open wrought-iron gates, and together they sat down on a cold, rusted bench.

"But I think we can solve this problem," he finally added.

Aha. Tom nodded, staring at Henrik with a combination of admiration and concern. He had gleaned the salient, unspoken point of Henrik's little monologue: he was doing Tom a favor. Using Interpol's resources to work on the sly. It could cost him his job. If not more. But George Niven was a very loyal friend, and if Henrik owed him a favor, this might be the closest he could come to paying George back. By helping Tom.

"Tell me," Tom breathed.

Henrik's eyes darted over the park, then came to rest in his lap. "I have a team of younger agents working after hours on this," he whispered. "They've hacked into the bank's mainframe. They're still working to debug the data. Some of it's scrambled, but it looks like there's a trail leading straight from Zurich to Moscow. It's a Russian account."

Tom felt a prickle of excitement. After losing the German thread, this was good news indeed. At any rate, it was better—a lot better—than nothing. "How soon?"

"We'll have confirmation in a matter of hours, I expect." Henrik looked him in the eye. "We're going to get him, Tom."

"I know. I know." Tom sighed.

For a moment the two men sat in silence. Tom watched a pigeon land on the head of a bronze statue nearby. The sculpture was splotched white from bird droppings and badly oxidized into an eerie blue. Who was the artist? Or the subject, for that matter? It looked like a copy of a Rodin, maybe: a common man depicted in classical terms, as opposed to a hero or a historical figure. Yes, Tom decided, this was just a man, his head tilted up, hands in the air, as if beseeching God. A man in pain, looking for an answer. Or maybe he was just a man going mad. A monument to human suffering. A representation of Tom himself.

He blinked, feeling the familiar, sandpapery itch of exhaustion in his irises.

Gaia. . . kidnapping. . . terrorist. . . DNA.

GaiakidnappingterroristDNAGaiakidnappingterrorist DNAGaia.

Gaia.

He'd run the disjointed words through his mind a thousand times since he'd heard them crackle on the train platform in Berlin. The missing pieces of the puzzle had been within his grasp, so close. And then the informant had been eliminated, leaving Tom with only a string of words, a snatch of some greater message that could be read a million ways. What did Loki's operations have to do with Gaia? And DNA? Was that in fact a reference to the genetic code? Or was it an acronym for some nefarious terrorist cell? Or a code name for some operation?

Kidnapping.

Well, that at least was easy. And so Gaia was under surveillance, though of course she didn't know it. Or at least Tom hoped she didn't. Because if she did, she'd shed the protection like snakeskin. She would never allow herself to be watched. She was too smart.

"You're not safe at a hotel, Tom," Henrik remarked. He removed a flat, silver case from his breast pocket. "You should stay with me. My wife, Charlotte, would be most pleased." He smiled, offered Tom a cigarette.

Tom shook his head. "You've gone to enough trouble on my behalf. I'll be fine." He stood up. "Right now my matchbox room at the Pension Arboire sounds like heaven." He smiled thinly. "At least no one would think to look for me there. It's all backpackers from Australia."

"No worries, mate," Henrik joked. He stood up, unfolding his long frame from the bench, a smile creasing the corners of his clear eyes. "I'll meet you there, tomorrow at 0900. We should have some solid information on your brother by then. If sooner, I'll make contact."

As Tom gripped Henrik's hand, he felt a swell of emotion so forceful, it almost overwhelmed him. He knew it was partially exhaustion. But that only magnified his genuine gratitude—a feeling he normally kept well hidden, like anyone else in the business. This man was putting himself on the line. Risking his job for someone he didn't even know. Of course, that was the way it had always been among agents—and Tom himself had done the same thing before. But that didn't detract from the fact that Henrik van de Meulen was helping Tom protect his child.

"Thank you," Tom murmured gruffly, averting his eyes. His wires were frazzled.

"Glad to be of service. Any friend of George. . . ." Henrik left the sentence hanging.

Tom stood and watched as Henrik walked through the wrought-iron gates of the park, rounded the corner, then disappeared. A light rain began to sprinkle. He wished he could get on the phone right now and thank George for putting him in touch with this man.

But they'd agreed to keep communication minimal for Gaia's own safety. And for Tom's.

Of course, even with the help of Henrik and his team, tracking Loki would be next to impossible. It was very likely Henrik wouldn't find anything at all, much less by nine o'clock the next day. But George had promised that Henrik was the best man for the job. Tracking money was his specialty.

Tom hurried from the park. He only hoped George was right.

". . . THUS THE GROUNDBREAKING

Snobs, Fruit Flies, Whatever

genetic sequencing of the fruit fly provides us with invaluable insight into who we are and what we're made of," the guest speaker intoned. "It's a key to the past."

Gaia chewed her thumbnail as the man cleared his throat and adjusted his glasses. He seemed nervous. And who could blame him? Most of the kids in this class would be psyched if he dropped dead. They were either thinking about lunch, wondering which rerun of *Dawson's Creek* would be broadcast tonight, or daydreaming about sex. She'd be surprised if anyone in this room had heard *half* his speech. She felt kind of sorry for the guy, actually—talking to a sea of bored, unimpressed kids. It didn't help that he was a classic professor type: a tiny, spindly man with eyes magnified behind giant glasses. He looked a bit like a fruit fly himself.

"Questions?" Mr. Dean, the new physics teacher, asked sharply. He cast a sour gaze across the room. "Dr. Forsyth has been generous enough to donate his valuable time to us. Now is your chance to ask a real biochemist about the Human Genome Project."

Gaia stared at her ragged fingernails. *Please don't call on me,* she prayed silently. *Please—*

"Yeah, I still don't get what a fruit fly has to do with, like, *anything*. And no offense, but basically, they're gross."

A couple of kids snickered.

Megan Stein. Gaia rolled her eyes. She didn't even have to look up. She would recognize that ditzy, irritating voice anywhere. Megan was the first and foremost FOH, Friends of Heather. A supersnob. A megabitch. And not to be cruel, but she wasn't exactly an intellectual giant.

"Megan, did you not hear one word of Dr. Forsyth's lecture?" Mr. Dean snapped. For once, Gaia empathized with his snippy, poker-up-the-ass tone. "All living organisms are connected. Mapping the entire genetic code for a living creature—the fruit fly—is the most important scientific endeavor since Einstein's work on the theory of relativity. It's what has enabled scientists to begin mapping the code of human life. It's of monumental . . ."

Gaia tuned the scene out. Snobs, fruit flies, whatever. She knew all about the genetic code. And Einstein's theory of relativity, too, for that matter. She was only in school these days because it was the one place where she didn't have to pay attention to anything. It was the one place where she could think—where she could sort through this mess with Uncle Oliver and figure out what the hell she was going to do with her future.

And, of course, it was the one place where she could see Ed.

She frowned. Actually, she could see Ed anytime, anywhere. But in school, surrounded by the usual cast of Village idiots, the awkward state of their relationship seemed to dissipate. A little bit, anyway. And she suddenly realized that she wasn't being completely honest with herself. There was another reason she came to school: it was safe. Ironically, she could pretend to be normal here.

Of course, it was all an elaborate charade. Drifting from class to class, listening to guest speakers, acting like things were okay, and going through bullshit details of life—all of it was based on denial. A waste of time, in the end. "Normal" life was for "normal" people. Like the fruit fly guy. Or Megan Stein. And even if abnormal people could occasionally partake of it, Gaia had no business being here. She was wasting *other* people's time as well. Nothing mattered except knowing the truth about Oliver. And her father.

"... a key to the past," the professor said again.

A key to the past. Gaia's mouth twisted into a small, grim smile. She needed a lot more than a fruit fly to unlock the secrets of *her* past—at least, as to how it related to her uncle and her father. But where was she going to get her information? Whatever one said, the other completely contradicted. They were identical twins but the exact opposite. In some ways Gaia couldn't even tell them apart anymore. She was too confused. As far as she knew, they might *both* be "Loki," the infamous terrorist.

But no—she couldn't give up hope. She couldn't allow herself to fall back into that cycle of doubt, hope, and hesitation. She had to stick to the facts. Just as she'd told herself a hundred times. Besides, Ed had helped her decide to stay put for now. That was a decision she intended to honor.

Maybe Oliver really did love her.

Maybe.

Gaia picked up her pen and absently scribbled the beginnings of a chart in her notebook:

Oliver on Oliver	_Dad on Oliver_
loves me	_incapable of love_
scapegoat	_terrorist ("Loki")_
victim	_pathological liar_

What the hell am I doing?

The pen slipped from her fingers and rolled across the page. This was supremely stupid. It didn't clarify a thing. She could go on forever and she still wouldn't see any patterns, any way of discerning the lies from the truth. She glanced at the two columns. The left was as plausible as it was outrageous, the right as absolutely true as it was false.

Pointless.

Disgusted, Gaia slipped her notebook into her messenger bag. Both Dean and the professor were facing the blackboard. Without a moment's hesitation she slunk silently out of the classroom, ignoring the curious, protesting stares of the other students. After all, she was just doing what they had been fantasizing about doing from the moment the class started.

She scanned the empty corridor. What she needed was. . .

Ed.

Right. Maybe they could just go eat. Not talk, just eat. Hot dogs. Doughnuts. Soda. When in doubt, junk food and zero conversation. Ed understood that better than anybody. Now, as long as he didn't mention Heather Gannis—

Gaia stopped herself in midthought.

A flash of something odd and unpleasant zigzagged through her stomach. Was it jealousy? No. Of course not. Sure, Gaia had experienced many jealous moments with Heather, but not over Ed. Not like this. This was new. This was almost. . . territorial. And uncomfortable.

And much more intense.

So what the hell was it?

Best not to answer. Gaia strode down the hall toward the exit. She had enough complication and confusion in her life already. She didn't need to throw Ed into the mix.

TOM CLIMBED THE LAST FLIGHT OF

The Wolf
stairs to his room at the Pension Arboire. His legs felt like lead. The building was too old for elevators—typical of old Brussels. Even though he'd awakened here this morning, he could barely remember what the room looked like, only that it was small and nondescript, like the pension itself. It was the kind of place where you could

hide when someone was on your tail. Or when you were trying covertly to stay on theirs.

He slipped his key in the lock and wondered if Loki's men had spotted him in the city. He was inclined to think so, although he prayed that he'd managed to duck and dive since Germany, that he hadn't been followed at all these past two days.

Oliver was better than that, though.

Yes, Tom had felt eyes on him, watching him. But maybe it was just his imagination (a euphemism for paranoia, to be sure). His mental faculties had certainly been impaired by exhaustion. Either way, it didn't hurt to be careful. Tom was relieved that both he and Henrik had kept a low profile today. It wasn't wise to meet in person. In fact, Tom had already made a decision: unless an emergency necessitated a rendezvous, he never intended to see Henrik's face again. At least, not until the mission was over. Meeting was an unnecessary risk, one that put both their lives in danger.

Tom shook his weary head as he closed the door behind him. Night had long since fallen, and the afternoon had brought only the tepid news that the agents working to debug the numbers of Loki's account had deciphered the first half of the code. Apparently they'd also detected a pattern to the encryption hurdles. Good, but not good enough. Not with all that was at stake. No doubt Loki had used a different sequence for the second half of the code. This was money, after all. Few things were sweeter to Loki.

Except Gaia.

Tom's face twisted as he wondered for the thousandth time what his brother wanted with his child. *Whatever it is, you'll never get her,* he swore in silent anger. *If I have to give my life to ensure it, I—*

He froze. Someone else was in the room.

A presence shifted in the darkness. Instinctively Tom reached for the small .22-caliber pistol in his breast pocket, then snapped on the light. Sitting on a corner of the twin bed was a powerfully built man with a pale complexion and eyes so light, they looked like they were made of blue glass. He wore a suit. An Armani. Loki's favorite brand. For a moment Tom and the man simply stared at each other. Then the man on the bed raised his hand and put a finger to his lips. "Shhh," he said.

In his lap he held a gun—a thirty-eight, with a long silencer.

Tom didn't hesitate. He jerked his own pistol at the man's head. "Get up," he commanded.

Suddenly the man's face transformed from a pale, impassive stare to an openmouthed, glazed look of fear. He didn't move. Tom heard a soft *thwap* behind him, to the left. A neat, red hole appeared in the man's forehead. His eyes seemed to glaze over. Again he simply stared at Tom, but there was no life behind his gaze. Blood trickled down his cheekbone, and he fell back on the bed.

Tom whirled around.

Henrik stood in the doorway, holding a pistol identical to the one that lay in the hands of the lifeless intruder. He was breathing heavily.

"How—" Tom began.

"Loki's on to you," Henrik panted, answering Tom's unspoken question. "We finished the traces on his account about an hour ago. When we saw funds being funneled to an account in Brussels, I got worried."

"Who was he?" Tom asked, glancing back at the body on the bed. A pool of blackish blood formed under the assassin's head, oozing onto the pillows.

"Wolfgang Flemmer," Henrik answered. He leaned against the door frame and wiped the sweat from his brow, still clinging to the pistol.

Tom's eyes narrowed. "The Wolf?"

Henrik nodded. "You know him?"

"Of course. A hit man. I've never seen him. I know he's been to trial three times in the last three years. No one's been able to pin anything on him. But. . . ." Tom exhaled and sat down in a chair. He felt dizzy, disoriented.

"We've got to go, Tom," Henrik murmured, looking warily through the window at the night sky. "It's not safe for you here."

"I know, I know." Tom nodded. Henrik was right, of course. If one of Loki's emissaries had found him here, more would follow. He sighed heavily and stood, then reached for the small bag of clothes he kept at the foot of the bed. He felt like he was moving in a dream; his body was functioning independently of his mind. "I just didn't know that the Wolf was in Loki's employ—"

"Don't worry about that," Henrik breathed, scanning the room quickly. "We have to get you out of here." He laid a gentle hand on Tom's shoulder and guided him toward the door. "You'll stay with us."

Tom shook his head, freezing in place. "Out of the question. I won't endanger your fam—"

"You don't have a choice. We've all put our lives on the line for others. That's our business. You know that George saved my life. More than once, in fact. This is how I will repay him. How I *must* repay him."

Tom was silent for a moment. He'd already guessed as much. He also knew that it was never wise to confuse personal matters with business, especially in their profession. Yet somehow it always happened. Always. Tom was guilty of it himself. And frankly, he needed all the help he could get right now. Loki's forces were closing in. So. He would regroup at Henrik's house, then be on his way—to a hotel, to a different city, anywhere. "All right," he said. "But I'll only stay for an hour."

Henrik nodded somberly. "We'll discuss that on the way," he said. He closed the door behind them on the dead assassin.

Gaia isn't the most subtle
girl on the block. But that's
always been fine by me. I'm not
the world's most subtle guy.
Which is why we became friends.
At least, I think that's why we
became friends. It might have
also had something to do with the
fact that I once stupidly tried
to save her from a bunch of skin-
heads—in a wheelchair no less—and
she took pity on me.

Wait—did I mention that I used
to be in a wheelchair?

Yes. Yes, I did.

Funny, isn't it? Somehow, in
some way, it all comes back to
the goddamned wheelchair.
Specifically, the lack thereof.

Gaia and I have dealt with our
fair share of respective bullshit
in our time. Another reason I
think we became friends. But usually I can read her. Usually if
she's got something on her mind,
I can tell if it's me or her dad
or Sam or whatever. And if it *is*
me that's yanking her chain, I

come right out and ask her why.
Or at least, that's what I used
to do.

These days, though, she
doesn't respond. She goes
through the motions. So do I. We
talk and joke and perform the
rituals of friendly interaction.
But then I catch her looking at
me strangely, and it's like she
thinks I'm another person. I
want to talk to her in those
moments. I want to say, "Stop
looking at me like I'm some ass-
hole you just met and don't
trust."

But of course, I never do.

I've recapped everything
we've said and not said, done
and not done in the last few
weeks, and I can't figure out
what the deal is. I mean sure, I
know there are days when Gaia
thinks I'm just another jerk in
a male-dominated, chauvinistic
world. Rarely, but it happens.
Or it used to, mostly when
Heather and I were trying to

test out the old "second-time's-the-charm" theory in the romance department. (By the way, that theory is complete crap.)

The point is, during all of these potholes in our friendship—even when Gaia wouldn't talk to me—I always knew what her beef was. Or had a vague idea. But now I'm confused. I don't even know how to define Gaia's vibe. It's some kind of self-conscious, distancing thing. And again, there's only one factor to which I can attribute it. Only one thing that's changed between us: I can walk.

Okay, make that limp. With crutches, no less. But after you've been in a wheelchair for a few years, limping becomes the equivalent of doing a wild jig—even with the pain.

Don't get me wrong. I know Gaia's happy for me. She's almost happier for me than I am for myself, if that's possible. But maybe she's still getting used to it. Sure. That must be it. She's just acclimating to the new Ed. The way astronauts have to acclimate to life in zero gravity or scuba divers have to acclimate to incredible underwater pressure. It takes time.

I should know. I'm acclimating to it myself.

So maybe that's the problem. I mean, a lot of times I feel like two people trapped in one body. Not in a scary, schizo, Jekyll-and-Hyde way—but something has definitely changed. Almost like the old me is watching the new me. Or the old me is watching the even *older* me. If that makes any sense.

Here's the existential question: Am I still the same me if I'm a different me? Am I somehow less myself now that I'm more my old self, back where Shred left off? And is this why Gaia feels alienated? Because the Ed Fargoness of her Ed Fargo is somehow bound up within the paraplegic state?

Jesus. Just thinking about it
gives me a headache. No wonder
all those existentialist poets
were so depressed.

He was dizzy
and unsure,
but he also
felt
weirdly **baking-**
clear. Like **soda**
all the shit **smile**
in his mind
had been
flushed down
a toilet.

"YOU GOTTA BE KIDDING ME," ED said. He leaned heavily on his crutches, grinning at Gaia as she dug into her pocket for a grubby wad of bills. "We're really going to the Brooklyn Botanical Gardens?"

Control-Freak Armor

Gaia arched an eyebrow. "This is part two of our City Parks and Recreation tour," she said. "Now, come on. You didn't think I dragged you all the way out here just so we could eat at Gray's Papaya, did you?"

"Well, actually. . . Brooklyn hot dogs *are* known for their higher concentration of grease and fat. They're right up your alley."

"That's funny," Gaia said in a dry voice. She headed toward the ticket booth, playfully waving her arms at the blue sky. An early spring breeze rustled her hair. "This isn't about grease and fat, Ed," she called over her shoulder. "It's about having a productive day. It's beautiful out. We can get some exercise *and* learn something."

Ed laughed, mostly because he hadn't seen Gaia Moore act playful since—when? Probably since playing truth or dare with Mary Moss. He shook his head, wiping that thought from his memory as he watched her hand over the money to the ticket guy. **Now was** definitely not the time for depression. "You sound like my mother," he replied. "Since when has health or education been a priority?"

Gaia rolled her eyes. Ed couldn't believe this. He was teasing her, like old times. And she was reacting normally. Amazing. Miracle of miracles! He didn't quite understand it, either. Was this all it took to part the curtain of uncertainty and awkwardness between them? A trip to the Botanical Gardens? Maybe the sodas they had drunk on the subway ride out here had been spiked with some kind of magical, healing potion. Either that or drugs. Because without warning, provocation, or discussion, things were suddenly easy again. And it couldn't have come at a better time. Heather had just sent him a letter. Needless to say, it had unsettled him. Okay, maybe that was an understatement. It had unsettled him in the same way an iceberg had unsettled the *Titanic*.

Dear Ed,

Since you won't talk to me, I've decided to write you. Please, please read this. You don't have to answer if you don't want to, but let me say what's on my mind even if I don't deserve to take up your time.

I know I've been wrong. I regret it. More than you can possibly know.

I love you, Ed. There. I said it. And because I

59

love you so much, I'm not letting myself off easy. It's hard to face up to what I did to you, but you have to believe that I know how wrong I was. It's all I think about. I've been trying to figure out how it is that I could be so selfish and self-righteous about your decisions when I've made such crummy ones myself. If it weren't for me, you never would have ended up paralyzed in the first place. But that didn't stop me from being mad at you when you refused to accept the insurance settlement. It makes me sick just to think about it. How could I have acted like that?

Actually, I know the answer. I acted like that because I'm really, really good at being in denial.

I'm not a bad person, though. You know that, don't you? I won't give up on us. Not after all that we've been through. I won't give up until you know that I've changed and that I want to prove it to you.

Love,
Heather

Ed shuddered involuntarily. He'd read the letter probably twenty times—although he'd memorized it word for word by about the sixth or seventh time through. It wasn't hard to draw a conclusion from it, either. No. Heather needed help. Of the therapeutic kind.

That's all there was to it. And he certainly wasn't the guy who could provide it. No, that kind of help required several degrees from major universities in various disciplines: psychiatry, psychopharmacology, et cetera. It was so strange. Ed had never imagined a time when he would *pity* Heather Gannis. But here he was. How could she be so unrealistic? They were *over*. Period. And after what she'd put him through at Sarabeth's the other day, they could never go back. He knew her control-freak armor was starting to wear thin, but he had no idea that she—

"Hello? Earth to Ed! We've lost all contact!"

"Huh?" Ed blinked. Gaia was standing at the turnstile, waving frantically. "Oh. Sorry."

He hobbled toward her as fast as he could. He was actually sort of getting the hang of this crutching thing. It was still painful, of course—and still frustrating (a nice way of saying embarrassing), especially since Gaia pretty much had to escort him through the turnstile as if he were eighty years old. But he was undeniably a biped now. It would only get better.

"Let's start with the Fragrance Garden," Gaia suggested, leading him down a path lined with benches shaded by giant old trees. "It's right over here." She pointed toward a small circle marked by rows of colorful petals and herb beds. "I hear it's really cool."

Ed nodded. "Yeah, we really should take time out to smell the flowers," he joked.

Gaia groaned. "I think you've been spending too much time at home," she said. "That sounds like the kind of joke a dad would make."

Ed opened his mouth, then closed it. He was going to rattle off some witty (hopefully witty, anyway) comeback about dads and jokes, but at the last second he decided to drop it. It was best not to pursue the "dad" line of conversation with Gaia. In fact, anything to distract her from thinking about her dad or her uncle would probably be a good thing.

Gaia paused at the entrance. "The following plants have particularly strong fragrances," she read from a sign. "Whether known for their medicinal properties or merely for their dreamy aromas. . . blah, blah, blah," she finished. She strode into the garden. "Let's find out for ourselves."

"I got a better idea," Ed said, lurching in front of her. He reached out to a small, flat-leaved bush, then crushed a leaf between his fingers and held it up to Gaia's nose, making sure to block the plaque from her line of sight. "Take a hit and guess the plant. For a dollar."

"A dollar? Whew, Fargo, you're a big spender." She closed her eyes and inhaled loudly. "Yum. I'd say. . . sage."

"You sure?" Ed smiled as Gaia had another whiff.

"Okay, lemon."

"Lemons grow on trees, Gaia."

"Thank you, Einstein. All right. I give up."

"Lavender," Ed told her with a snicker. "God, Gaia, how many girls don't know what lavender smells like?"

Gaia opened her eyes and shot him a sarcastic smile. "Girls like me. Girls who don't have lavender pillows in their underwear drawer." She thought for a moment. "Girls who don't actually *have* an underwear drawer." The smile vanished. Her head drooped. In an instant, out of nowhere, she seemed down, preoccupied. "What do you say we go get a sugar fix? I packed a couple of candy bars."

Ed nodded, not wanting to question the sudden shift in mood. He should have known that the levity wouldn't last. Gaia was a wreck these days, a chameleon—her emotions changing color without warning. *So much for the healing properties of plants,* he thought. But a glucose infusion might help. He'd seen it before. If they could chill out long enough for her to stuff her face, then they could recapture the just-like-old-times vibe. It was worth a shot. He followed Gaia back out onto the path.

"How about down there?" she asked. She pointed to the Japanese Garden: an immaculate arrangement of old willow trees surrounding a small pond filled with koi the size of torpedoes.

Again Ed simply nodded. They sat down side by side in the grass, which took some doing—a lot of fumbling and hopping and assisting—but finally he was on his butt, and it was a huge relief. Gaia reached into her bag and dug out some squishy Milky Way bars, one of which she unceremoniously tossed to him.

For a while they said nothing. There was only the sound of chewing and of water lapping quietly next to them.

"You gotta love Brooklyn," Gaia mumbled finally. She lay down flat on her back and stared up at the tree. "Hey. Check this out."

Ed crumpled the candy wrapper in his fist and lay down beside her, his mouth still full of chocolate. *Hmmm.* She had a point. The view was pretty trippy. The green willow leaves were like a giant, torn umbrella, with the snatches of sky shining like blue ribbons. He finished swallowing and turned slightly, stealing a peek of Gaia in profile. From this angle she looked com-pletely at peace. Yup, it all came down to sugar.

She was very still, gazing up at the sky, her breath light and even. He was close enough to see the light freckles playing at the bridge of her nose. She closed her eyes. He could just lean over and—

And what?

Ed swallowed. He felt hot. The silence between them dragged on, seeming to stretch into an eternity. He couldn't stop what was happening to him. He was moving closer. Just a fraction of an inch—but still. . . it was almost like an out-of-body experience, like he was just a marionette and someone else was pulling the strings. He couldn't stop. He was going to—

He jerked back his head. His heart was thudding like a gong.

"Are things really over with Heather?" Gaia asked out of nowhere.

The question sliced through the still air. His pulse was racing now. Why would she mention Heather? She opened one eye. Had she felt what Ed felt? No. She was just pulling a classic Gaia: bringing up the most awkward and painful subjects without a second thought. He propped his head up on his elbow, forcing himself to breathe evenly. "Yeah. We're through. Heather is out of my life."

Part of him felt good saying it. But another part felt a pinch of guilty pain. Words from the letter scrolled through his mind, and he fought to block them out. They could never change the way he felt. She'd lied to him for two years. A lie of omission, no doubt, but still a lie. And the fact that her own obsession with status had led directly to his accident. . . her newfound confessional honesty was probably about as authentic as Madonna's English accent.

Okay, maybe that was overly cruel. Maybe that was just anger talking. Heather *was* sorry. It didn't change what she'd done, but at the very least, it prevented Ed from hating her completely. He could tell from her words that she was suffering. And that didn't make him particularly proud or pleased.

So put it out of your mind, Ed ordered himself. He needed to stay with the here and now. Going back was a road to nowhere. `Crutch forward!` Yes. That was the motto. Even if it hurt. Even if he fell flat on his goddamned face. It was forward or nothing.

"How about you and Sam?" Ed asked. Might as well put it out there. `One proverbial can of worms had already been opened.` Gaia had brought up the *H* word twice in one day. So the *S* word didn't seem like overstepping the mark.

"It's over," Gaia muttered, her gaze fixed to the sky. Her voice was low. She swallowed. "I never thought. . . ." Gaia shrugged. "Feelings change, I guess."

Ed didn't say a word. Truth be told, he was too shocked to respond. *Wow.* That was the most Gaia had ever confided to Ed about Sam. Ever. But it was okay. He didn't need to say anything. Not that he'd ever really known how to broach the Sam subject, anyway. The fact that Sam had gone out with Heather before Gaia complicated matters enough. But Gaia didn't need to say anything, either. Sam was part of their shared past. Their friendship was picking itself up and dusting itself off. Or maybe they were entering some new phase—

Just then Gaia turned, and Ed caught her eye. Something about the way she looked at him stopped his thoughts in their tracks. Was it his imagination? Or *was* there something new there, something different?

No. Gaia flicked her eyes away and sat up. She brushed some leaves from her hair. His heart sank. Except that when she turned to look at Ed, to help him up, the look was still there. He couldn't define it. Maybe it was nothing at all. So why did he felt like he'd just ridden the roller coaster at Coney Island instead of lying under a willow tree—expending about as much physical effort as a pebble in a Zen rock garden?

And then it hit him.

He was dizzy and unsure, but he also felt weirdly clear. Like all the shit in his mind had been flushed down a toilet. *When all of this is over,* he vowed. By "this" he meant Gaia's current state of being. Yes, he would take action when the giant swirl of debris and heartache that circled her like a twister had passed. If it ever did. But. . . *when all of this is over, I'm going to tell her how I really feel about her.*

He stole a glance at her as she picked up their candy wrappers and stuffed them into her messenger bag. Yes, he would come clean. When the time was right. When she could handle the truth. What was the worst that could happen? She could reject him. That was the worst. Tell him he was freaking crazy to imagine the two of them as anything other than just friends.

And so what if that happened? He had pretty much always lived in the shadow of Gaia's unspoken rejection. It was a pain he knew well.

"YOU'RE SURE YOU WANT ANOTHER scotch, buddy?"

Sam glowered up at the bartender. Then he flashed a lopsided smile. Everything was spinning in delirious harmony. From where he sat slumped on a stool in the darkness at. . . what was the name of this place again?. . . wherever, some dump in the East Village that served minors; anyway, the sour-looking, thirty-year-old slacker bartender looked more like two guys than one—

Nauseating Smog of Booze

"I think you should drink some coffee instead."

"No, no, iss fine," Sam slurred, shaking his head. He slapped the bar with his palm: the international symbol for another round. "'S not a problem."

No. Having one more drink would definitely *not* be a problem. Sure, he'd gotten into trouble drinking in the past. But he knew how to handle it now. Just like he knew how to handle darkness and misery and depression. He was an expert. *Practice makes perfect,* he thought—and hiccuped.

The bartender shook his head with a disgusted snort. "Last one," he grumbled, but he reached for the bottle.

"Thanks . . ." Sam was going to say, *Thanks, man,* but it was too much effort. He was half dead. Too drunk to care if he kept on drinking, and too drunk to know what else to do. It wasn't even eight o'clock—

Shit!

He laughed. He couldn't help it. Life *could* get worse. Of course it could! Almost immediately the soft edges of his buzz hardened into a moment of clarity. Sam's eyes were tracking the figure walking through the door even before his brain caught up with his vision. Yup. It was him, all right: sweatpants, Tom Cruise hair, that perennial, baking-soda smile varnished to his face. . . your regular Mr. RA Next Door, your classic best buddy, your Josh Kendall.

What a treat.

Without thinking, Sam lowered his face to his arms. Darkness. If ostriches could hide this way, maybe he could, too. Maybe he was invisible right now. Maybe Josh would walk right past him and leave.

"Sammy, bro!" Josh sang out. He slapped Sam's back.

Nope. *No such luck.* Sam hiccuped again. For a second he was worried he might puke all over the two of them. Which would be funny. He kept his face buried in the crook of his arm.

"Yo," Josh muttered with a snicker. "Letting it all out, huh? Slamming 'em solo?"

Finally Sam dug his bleary eyes out of his sleeve

and blinked up at the face he hated so much. It was pretty remarkable: not even the nauseating smog of booze overload could block out that hatred.

"You. . . you got tha' right," Sam said slowly, trying desperately to enunciate his words. "So why don' you leave me alone?"

Josh sighed. "Wish I could. No can do." He dropped a small package wrapped in bubble wrap and silver duct tape on the counter beside Sam's scotch.

"I'm off du. . . duty," he said coldly. "The asser iss no."

"The *what* is no?" Josh asked, grinning.

Sam scowled and reached for his drink. "Th' answer!" he barked. He tried to slug it down in one gulp, but half the scotch ended up on his face and shirt.

"This package has to be delivered within the hour," Josh said, as if he hadn't heard him.

Sam felt it building then. The fury in his gut. Pistons fired in his heart; heat radiated down his arm and into his fist—the fist now itching to rearrange Josh Kendall's facial bone structure.

"I said. . . *no!*" Sam roared.

A couple of heads turned. Just the other drunks at the bar. What did they care?

"You said no," Josh repeated. He spoke quietly, calmly. "And how many times do we have to go through this, Sam? You say no, I say yes. You refuse, and I threaten your sorry ass with jail. Or maybe we have to go a notch higher. You tell me to go screw myself, and I tell you the various ways in which your girlfriend will be killed if you disobey orders. You know I just have to say the word and it's done. So in fact, you say yes. Always yes. "

Sam swallowed. Never mind the fact that Gaia wasn't his girlfriend anymore. Occasionally, very occasionally, Josh would drop the buddy act and let his true colors show—those of a cold, calculating, and utterly mysterious killer. The back of Sam's throat felt as raw as a steak. Something burned there. Was it whiskey or tears? Why not slit it and find out?

Josh patted Sam on the shoulder. "Now sober up. And get your ass to Queens."

Sam didn't move. He put his elbows down on the counter. He closed his eyes. His head swam. He breathed in the darkness. Maybe if he wished long and hard enough, he could stay that way—stay still long enough so that his heart eventually slowed and stopped. And then, nothing but sleep and blackness. Why not? It wasn't as if he had anything to live for. School? He barely went to class. His grades were in a free fall. Friends? None left. People he knew tended to avoid him now; he looked like a wreck. Family? He hadn't spoken to his own parents in weeks.

Besides, if there was one thing this nightmare had

taught him, it was that anything was possible. Absolutely anything.

TOM NEVER EVEN BOTHERED TAKING

Fresh Footprints

off his coat. If he did so, Henrik might try to convince him to stay. Henrik's wife, Charlotte, was certainly making an effort. She kept asking Tom if he wanted coffee, a bite to eat, anything. But Tom wouldn't even allow himself to get a good look at her. When he'd walked through the door, something about her—the cheekbones? the white nape of her neck?—had instantly reminded him of Katia. And he couldn't afford to let his emotional armor crack. Not now. He had to ignore her, even at the risk of appearing rude.

Maybe he would get a chance to explain himself one day. But not tonight. It was simply best to stand in the hall of the cozy apartment and stare at Henrik as he called Interpol from an outdated phone-fax-copier unit on a side table.

Tom had smiled when he'd first seen the clunky old machine on entering the apartment. Most

European agents he knew kept these machines by their front doors. That way they were in a position to move quickly should any vital information arrive. It harkened back to days past, when things were simpler, when the enemy was clear-cut.

He wasn't smiling now.

The conversation was in Dutch, but Tom could understand every word. Evidently one of Henrik's hackers had found a promising lead: a confirmation on some numbered accounts in the former Soviet bloc. But then last time Loki had led him on a wild-goose chase. Tom chewed his lip. Just because they could trace Loki's numbers didn't mean the numbers themselves were real. Still, either way, Tom had no choice but to take each new piece of information seriously. And to keep hoping.

Henrik hung up.

"They've cracked the code, Tom," he whispered excitedly. "They're faxing us the information right now."

Tom swallowed. "They know where he is?"

"We haven't found him yet, but we've got some big footprints. And they're fresh."

The phone rang again, and the other parts of the machine whirred to life. Henrik caught the printout as it came through. His eyes narrowed, flashing over the page. "There are transfers to several different people," he murmured. "But there's a major monthly deposit—" He broke off, frowning.

"What?" Tom demanded.

Henrik handed over the page. "An account in Chechnya. First of the month without fail. It's in the name Igor Vasilyevic. My men ran some checks. He's a retired physicist, formerly the head of a large nuclear arms plant in Georgia—which was officially closed down in the 1980s."

Tom shook his head. His mind raced. *Chechnya. Inert nuclear arms plants.* The last lead on Loki had been an illegal weapons factory in the Sudanese desert that manufactured anthrax. Yet that had turned cold. Either that was a decoy or this was—or Loki had outwitted them again. Was it just another red herring, or was this real? At least the anthrax lead had seemed in the right camp. Biological warfare was consistent with the informant's few bits of insider information. *DNA. . . .*

But a retired Russian nuclear physicist in Chechnya?

"PLEASE LEAVE A MESSAGE AFTER the beep," Sam's gruff, recorded voice commanded.

Heather clutched the phone to her ear for a second, then slammed it

Bubbly New Airhead

down on the hook. Her heart pounded. She couldn't bring herself to speak.

"Heather?" Mrs. Gannis called from downstairs. "Heather, honey! Dinner!"

"I'll be there in a minute," Heather mumbled, knowing very well her mother couldn't hear her.

"Don't let it get cold!" her mom added. Her voice trilled.

That goddamned cheerfulness. Heather's jaw tightened. She preferred her mom the way she used to be—back when she was still panicked about money and Phoebe's anorexia and all the rest of it. Yes, this bubbly new airhead was definitely worse. Not a moment passed without her mother's euphoria breaking through. It was depressing. And alienating. *And not real.* It was like air freshener in a public bathroom; it only made the stench worse. Heather lay back on the pillows and stared up at the ceiling. There was no way that even in her darkest hours, even during the worst pits of hell she'd dragged herself through, she'd ever been quite this miserable.

This was a record.

Tears glittered in the corners of her eyes. She blinked them back. What was worse? Losing Ed or knowing that she deserved to lose him? A real tiebreaker, that one. Actually, the worst part of the whole thing was that Heather couldn't talk to anybody about her problems. She had no one. None of her friends had ever understood what she saw in Ed. . . nor had they known anything about her family troubles. And when it came right down to it, they didn't really give a shit about anyone unless they were having fun.

It was all ephemeral. There was no point in getting used to any of the feel-good vibrations permeating the Gannis home. Mom's happy face wasn't fooling Heather, nor was her father's stellar new job. Heather knew all about superficial smiles. Underneath, they were ravaged. And yeah, Phoebe was home and "eating"—if you could call scarfing a few bits of radicchio eating—but how long would that last? Heather knew firsthand it could all be gone in an instant. Even *if* her father really did have a great job and even *if* Phoebe's lettuce leaves signified a desire to live, it could all change with the weather. Here today, gone tomorrow. Like Ed. Like her friends.

Heather punched redial. She hung up before the first ring. What the hell was she doing? Calling Sam Moon was just plain weird. Her ex-boyfriend. Gaia Moore's boyfriend. *Don't think about her!* Heather silently screamed. No, bringing Xena, Warrior Bitch into the equation wasn't helping any. And besides, hideous as it was to contemplate, it wasn't relevant. Sam could date anyone he liked. Because the truth of it was that Heather only wanted a shoulder to cry on. She only wanted to talk. And Sam Moon had always been a good listener.

They had history together. That should count for something. Maybe he could give her some advice. On her family. He knew them well, and he would at least understand the tensions going on. And maybe enough time had elapsed since their breakup for him to be impartial about Ed.

Nah, scrap that. That was pushing it. But her family. . . Sam would be sympathetic. He'd know the right thing to say, wouldn't he?

He'd help her figure out a game plan. Heather sniffed and hit the redial button one more time. There was only one way to find out.

I'm a liar.

It's a description of me that I thought would never fit. But yesterday at the Botanical Gardens, I told Ed that things were over between me and Sam.

Why would I lie?

Maybe because I'm hoping I *can* get over him. For the longest time I didn't believe that Sam could really see anything in someone like me. But then for a brief, golden moment I stopped caring about the mechanics of our chemistry. And I realized that true chemistry is, in fact, alchemy: a magical blending of unknown properties that cannot be measured or even understood. It just happens. It's a potion that intoxicates. We scoff, but when it happens to us, we suck it right down. Or at least, I did.

But that was a long time ago. Or at least it feels like a long time ago.

Sam tells me he loves me. It means nothing. Words deprived of

GAIA

actions are just words. Take my
father: he tells me he loves me,
too. I have twenty pounds of letters he wrote to me over the
years he was AWOL, letters filled
with words like *love* and *always*
and *forever*. But it wears kind of
thin when you find yourself
alone. With nothing but a letter
filled with *love* and *always* and
forever, when what the letter
really says is "good-bye."

Promises, promises. Dad and
Sam. They're so similar, they're
starting to blend together, a
painful blur of words without
action, sudden random disappearances, and absentee love. Then
again, Dad is gone and Sam is
still here, at least physically.
Which does make me wonder if I
shouldn't at least try to sal-
vage what's left of me and Sam.
After all, I've put so much into
it. It would be nice to come
away with more than squat.
Especially since I can't stop
thinking about the guy.

I wish there were some way to
rewind—to go back to the time
when Sam and I would have rather
cut off our limbs than let lies
come between us. But I can't go
back because Sam won't go there
with me. I look at him and see
that he's changed. He's no longer
the guy I fell in love with. He's
somewhere else. Someone else.
He's like a bad actor imitating
himself. Keanu Reeves as Sam
Moon.

And I'm not the same girl with
him, either. I have my own lies,
my own secrets.

Come to think of it, I'm an
actress myself.

Ontology.

The study of "being." I learned that in MacGregor's lit and philosophy seminar just before we started reading Camus, while I was still Ed of the Wheelchair. It sounded like a tub of crap at the time— all these extremely anal scholars splitting hairs over what it means to "be"—but now here I am doing the same thing because I'm walking. One moment I'm The Cripple—and then hey, presto, King Crutch.

Not that this has anything to do with anything at all. But that's philosophy for you: the rambling thoughts of a bunch of old guys who had way too much time on their hands.

I wish I could just talk to Gaia about what's going on between us. I wish I could put my questions on the table and hash them out in our old, blunt way. But it's too stilted between us for me to get anything real out of her. We can talk, but only

about external problems. Not
about us. We can't be frank about
our feelings—not that I ever
really have been about my own
feelings with her. But maybe
that's the root of Gaia's head
change: maybe I've subconsciously
been revealing the feelings I've
always had for her, and maybe
she's picked up on it.

Not a good thought. I've been
squashing those feelings ever
since she first made it clear she
didn't like me that way. And it's
been cool for the most part.
Okay, not "cool"—but at least
we've had some kind of relationship. I think I've done a good
job. But maybe since I've been so
happy/terrified/self-involved
with the new me, I've let it all
hang out. I sure as hell hope
not. Been there, done that. I
don't *feel* like I've been sending
Gaia hidden messages. But who
knows? I'm not exactly "myself"
these days. Ontologically speaking, that is.

And what happened to the decision I made at the Botanical Gardens? The big, bold, life-changing decision to finally confess to Gaia that I've pretty much been in love with her from day one? I guess it went the way philosophy always seems to go. What I mean is: in theory, philosophy is a nice idea, but the second you're back in the real world, you pretty much forget about it. It doesn't do you much good. In fact, it scares the shit out of you.

Maybe globe-trotting with uncle Oliver wouldn't be so bad. Anything was better than **the sewer** this endless parade of rejection.

"THERE'S A MAN HERE TO SEE YOU."

Awful Memories

Gaia froze as she closed the apartment door behind her. Olga, the Moss family's cook and housekeeper, was standing in the foyer. She smiled pleasantly. Gaia barely noticed that Olga had spoken in Russian. A flash of adrenaline coursed through her veins. It was ironic: she was feeling something close to fear, or as close to fear as she could get. Over a visitor. Not that she was truly afraid, of course. Or even all that surprised. It was more that she was sickened. This place was supposedly a safe haven, a sanctuary. The outside world wasn't supposed to intrude.

"Who?" Gaia whispered, her eyes darting toward the living room. She couldn't see around the corner, but if it was a man, it was probably one of two people, her father or her uncle. And she was in no condition to see either of them. Not when she was so confused on so many fronts. She still hadn't come close to making up her mind about her uncle's proposition. Oliver had said he'd give her time to think. . . and her father, well, her father was the same old question mark he'd always been.

Could it be Sam, then? But then Olga would have used the word for *boy*.

85

"I don't know who he is," Olga replied, shrugging and returning to the kitchen. "He won't say."

Oliver. Gaia swallowed. Definitely her uncle. Only Oliver would be so secretive. She took a deep breath and forced herself to march into the living room. Maybe when she saw his face, she'd have a clearer picture—

"George?"

Whoa. Gaia hadn't been expecting George Niven. But then, why not? Technically, he was still her legal guardian. Of course he'd stop by to check up on her. And she couldn't help but feel more than mildly disappointed. *He* was concerned for her welfare, but clearly her blood relatives were not. She forced a smile as she sat across from him. It wasn't easy. He looked terrible, as if he were sick. His hair was grayer. Sunlight poured through the windows, casting shadows on skin that was as pale as milk. And he was thin—too thin in his suit. His dry lips twitched as he tried to force a smile in return.

"Hello, Gaia," he murmured.

Poor George, Gaia thought. Seeing him filled her with blackness every time; it dredged up too many awful memories. Ella's body, in a puddle of blood. That decrepit apartment on the Lower East Side. Sam's betrayal. George was somebody she didn't want to confront. He was just too sad, too pitiful—a shell of a guy who never deserved what life had dealt him, a decent man who went out of his way for others and somehow always got shit in return. The truth was, Gaia didn't know how to handle it. Part of her wanted to reach out to him—but guiltily, the larger part wished that he would just disappear.

"How are you?" Gaia asked in the silence.

"Fine," he said.

She stared at him. She knew why he was here. He wanted her to come back to Perry Street and live with him in the brownstone. She would sooner live in the sewer. She couldn't even bear to imagine it: Gaia and George, two wounded birds. A regular party.

"George, listen, I really appreciate—"

"You need to come with me," George stated in an oddly cold voice. "Your father asked *me* to take care of you. I'm your legal guardian. You're not safe here."

Gaia's phony smile faded. "I make my own decisions," she said. "I'm sorry. I know you're caught in the middle of this. But if he cares so much about my safety and well-being, he'd be here with me now. Besides, I *am* safe." She glanced toward the living-room window, mostly to avoid looking at George's desperate, anxious eyes.

"Your father is a good man," George breathed. There was a fresh urgency in his voice. "Someday you'll understand why he had to go. You have no idea how—" He broke off suddenly and stood. "I can't discuss this. You need to come with me, though. That's all I can say."

"Well, that isn't good enough," Gaia muttered. She turned to him, then quickly turned away again. There was too much pain and vulnerability in that face. But there was tenderness, too. She just wanted this little visit to end as fast as possible. *A good man. Your father is a good man.* Sure, he was. He was a liar. A man who chose his job over his family. A man who killed people for a living.

George stepped toward her. "Gaia, I—"

There was a muffled, high-pitched ringing. He withdrew slightly and fished a cell phone out of his pocket. Gaia's eyes narrowed. He didn't say one word. He simply opened the cell phone, listened, and closed it. But a change had taken place. What little color remained in his cheeks had vanished completely.

"What is it?" Gaia asked.

"I'm sorry," he stated. He shoved the phone back into his pocket. "I have to go. Gaia—this conversation isn't over. I just. . . ." He didn't finish. Instead he simply strode from the living room.

A moment later the apartment door slammed behind him.

Gaia sat still. And then, surprising herself, she laughed. It was pretty much all she could do at this point. Yeah, well, maybe George didn't care for her as much as she'd thought. He'd gone the way of every single other man in her life. A fortuitous phone call, a surprise letter, an e-mail (it didn't matter which), and—*boom!*—they were all gone. One little push was all it took to send them scurrying out of her life. Any excuse to split. No wonder George and her father were such close friends. They both had their list of priorities very, very straight. And Gaia's name was nowhere on it.

Screw it, she thought. Maybe globe-trotting with Uncle Oliver wouldn't be so bad. Anything was better than this endless parade of rejection.

Useless Pessimism

"PLEASE TRY TO RELAX, TOM," Charlotte van de Meulen pleaded. "Just have a seat in the living room. Have some brandy."

Tom shook his head. He wasn't budging from the front hall. Allowing Henrik to leave the apartment without him had been stupid. He was trapped here, alone with the man's wife, in this place—endangering her. But Henrik had insisted that he go alone. He'd promised he'd only be gone for ten minutes. And now. . . .

Tom's eyes flashed to his watch again. Nine minutes and forty-three seconds had already expired. How did he let himself fall into these kinds of situations? The old Tom had been in control. Enigma, the antiterrorist expert, would never had allowed this to happen. Enigma would have put as much distance as possible between himself and these people.

"George is watching your daughter," Charlotte said comfortingly, as if reading his mind. She placed a snifter of brandy on the side table beside the fax machine. "Even as we speak."

"I know," he whispered. Yes, he knew that George had gone to retrieve Gaia from the Moss home. It was about time. The Mosses were good people, but they had no idea how to protect his daughter. Of course, he still hadn't received confirmation that Gaia was in fact back at Perry Street. But it would come soon. He was sure of it. He couldn't allow himself to be distracted by conjecture. George would accomplish his mission. He *had* to accomplish his mission. Just as Tom had to accomplish his.

Time's up.

The numbers on his watch shifted. Ten minutes had elapsed. His fingers itched to dial George, to dial Henrik. But making a phone call wasn't just risky; it was suicidal. Loki was probably counting on Tom to break down and use his cell phone. No doubt the trace had been in place for days, waiting to be triggered. All Tom had to do was dial, and minutes later assassins would burst through the door—

"Don't be so hard on yourself," Charlotte soothed. "You're doing what you can. And your daughter will be fine. A parent can't be everywhere at once. Guilt does not help."

"Are you speaking from experience?" Tom asked grimly.

"In fact, I am. Our own daughter, Johanna, was almost taken from us several years back. Interpol had captured the head of a so-called liberation army in South America. Henrik was the arresting agent. The terrorists then sent a small army after our daughter. We had to hide her all over the place. We have her in boarding school in Switzerland because we think she's safer there."

Tom didn't respond. He could only shake his head once more. Some life they all led. He barely even remembered the days when the Agency had truly meant something to him. When it had been about saving lives. Because what did saving lives mean if you couldn't save your own child? He was wallowing in useless pessimism, though. He absently reached for the brandy and took it down in one gulp.

"George *is* watching her," he said out loud, to convince himself. "No one can get past him."

The front door burst open. Tom instinctively reached for his gun, then saw that it was Henrik.

"Your lucky day, Tom," Henrik panted breathlessly, his overcoat swooping behind him. He shut the door and grinned. His eyes shone. "We've struck gold. Tapped into the physicist's phone line in Chechnya. Loki is to meet him there tomorrow."

Tom's skin prickled with anticipation. "You're sure?"

"As sure as we'll ever be. We have to get going if we're going to get there ourselves."

"Now?" Charlotte piped up behind Tom. Her voice was tremulous.

Henrik nodded. "We're driving to Amsterdam. Our flight leaves tonight. From there we will fly to Chechnya. It would be quicker to fly through Brussels International, but if Loki's men are watching, that's the first place they'll look."

Tom didn't need to hear another word. His hand was already reaching for the doorknob.

"WAKE UP, SAMMY."

Sam opened one bleary eye and found himself looking directly into Josh's perfectly polished grin. He immediately winced. Even the slightest movement hurt. His head was ringing like a gong. He could still feel scotch burning through his blood.

He licked his dry lips. Mistake. His tongue was like Velcro.

"Time to rise and shine, bro. Hate to do it, but I've got something I need you to run over to Chelsea for me."

Sam turned to the digital clock on his bedside table. 5:45 A.M. Was the son of a bitch out of his thick skull? Sam could barely *move*. If he did, he'd vomit all over the place. Somehow, even in his sickly drunken state, he'd delivered some package to Queens only hours before. . . or did he just dream that? It didn't matter. Dream or no dream, there wasn't a chance in hell he'd be getting up and doing another errand. Not now.

Not ever, his inner voice pounded.

"Get out," Sam muttered hoarsely. His chapped lips cracked, and he winced again. His tongue darted out of his mouth, and he tasted blood. "Get out of my room."

Josh's shiny smile disappeared, replaced by a dead glare. Then, just as quickly, the smile resurrected itself—as if a rain cloud had simply drifted momentarily in front of a bright, scorching sun. "I get it," he said. "It's our new ritual. You say no, I say yes. You finally give in. It's cute, Sammy. Kinda like flirting. Now, if I didn't know you better, I might think you were—"

"I said get out. I need my sleep."

Sam figured he should have been surprised at himself. His voice sounded so calm, so deliberating. So sober. But even though his half-drunk brain was barely functioning, he knew deep down that he was long past surprising himself. All the lies and acting had irrevocably damaged him. He had a hundred different personalities, and any one of them might reveal itself at any time. He had about as much control over his mind as an airline passenger did over a flight. Why not let the drunken rebel in him speak? So what if it was stupid? At least it *felt* right.

"I'll write down the address for you," Josh said.

Sam smiled up at him. "You'll have to kill me before you get me to do another delivery for you, Kendall. Got it. . . *bro?*" He felt like shit, but he felt pretty damn good, too. Josh actually looked *pissed*. No more slick boy. He was at a loss for words. For once in his miserable life. Maybe, just maybe, Josh Kendall wasn't the big wheel Sam thought he was. Maybe he was just some petty drug runner. Some lowlife trying to make a sleazy buck.

Ignoring the brutal pain of the hangover, Sam swung his legs out of bed. He didn't take his eyes off Josh. He crossed the room and held his bedroom door wide open. He had to cling to this lie as long as possible: the belief that Josh *wasn't* connected to a force greater than anything Sam could imagine. Because Sam knew it was true. Josh could summon a laser gun sight at will. One was probably trained on Sam's temple right now.

"Kill me or leave me," Sam heard himself say. "That's my final offer."

Josh's smile returned. "Fine. Have it your way."

Sam's grip tightened on the doorknob. Josh was reaching for his hip. The movement of his hand was very quick. The room started to spin. Sam could feel invisible energy rushing through his limbs, his brain—the adrenaline pushing him to get out, to get the hell out now. But instead he just watched as Josh withdrew a small pistol. Was he drunk? Was he awake, asleep?

You're awake. You're awake. There's a psychopath in your room.

He turned. Not fast enough. A splintering pain pierced his lower back. Sam staggered forward, clinging to the door for support. He went down while he was still trying to process what had happened. *Have I been shot?* The floor rose up to answer him. Sam's last thought was that he'd always hated that puke-orange carpet. Luckily it transformed into a thick white wall into which he could sink forever and ever.

Memo

To: L
From: S
Date: March 6
File: 002
Subject: Enigma

Travel plans confirmed. Security in position.

From: gaia13@alloymail.com
To: smoon@alloymail.com
Time: 1:10 A.M.
re: Confused

Hi,

Okay, I'm going to regret this tomorrow. But
this time I haven't had any wine. I'm perfectly
lucid. At least about this. I just wanted to say
that I'm sorry about the way I acted in the park
the other night. I guess I kind of wasn't being
myself. Whoever "myself" is.

Can you answer that question, Sam?

Not about me, I mean. About you.

Boy, I'm articulate these days, aren't I? I
guess all that skipping school is starting to
have an effect on me. Anyway, whenever I feel
like I don't make any sense, I revert back to the
trusty old chess metaphor. Specifically, I feel
like we're playing a game of chess that hasn't
been finished. We've both just walked away from
the table, unsatisfied. I've gotten a few steps
closer to your queen, but I haven't been able to
make the decisive move.

This isn't chess, though, is it?

All I'm saying is that I want to talk. One
last time. Just to settle this. If you don't want
to talk, fine. Game over. Draw.

And remember, I won't judge you. Whatever it is you've done or are hiding, I've probably done a lot worse.

Gaia

From: gaia13@alloymail.com
To: shred@alloymail.com
Time: 1:15 A.M.
re: Don't laugh

Hey, Ed,

Okay, here's a weird thought that just popped into my head: Do you want to come over and have dinner with Mary's mom and me tomorrow night? The food will be very unhealthy and delicious, I promise.

G$

He tried to
bolt upright
but couldn't.
He *knew*
this face **near-**
somehow—and **death**
experience
it was not
the face of
God.

CROUCHING ON THE FLOOR IN THE

back of a car—particularly in these tiny French numbers, the Deux Chevaux, which were really no bigger than go-carts—could never be called comfortable. But comfort was the last thing on Tom's mind. He was safe. Or at least safer than he would be sitting in the seat, with his head a moving target for some sniper. His bones rattled with every bump. No doubt he'd be aching by the time they reached Amsterdam.

Crossed Wives

"You okay back there?" Henrik asked from the driver's seat.

"Fine."

As the car curved around corners and sped toward the highway, Tom's thoughts sped as well. It was going to be tricky piecing together exactly what Loki's interests in Chechnya were. If there even were any.

"What has this physicist been doing since the fall of the Soviet Union?" Tom asked.

"What everyone else has," Henrik mused grimly. "Trying to profit from the leftover scraps of the cold war." He sighed. "I'm sure that's why Loki has been paying him."

"Maybe," Tom said. "It's likely just another decoy." Yes, a sale of nuclear weapons on the black market certainly didn't fit with the strange message the informant had been so desperate to impart in Berlin. *DNA. . . kidnapping. . . Gaia. . . terrorist. . .* For the thousandth time the words ricocheted through Tom's skull like bullets. But maybe *that* had been a decoy.

Or was Loki planning on bartering Gaia for some reason?

Under other circumstances, Tom might have laughed aloud at that possibility. But there was nothing remotely humorous about this situation. Such wild cut-and-paste versions of the informant's message had to be considered. Every possibility was plausible. The absurd had always provided inspiration for Loki. Tom knew that better than anyone. All those years Loki had spent underground, he had been hatching something grand and obscene. He was nothing if not predictable in his unpredictability.

"We're out of the city now," Henrik said. "I think it's safe to come back up front."

Flashes of countryside whipped past the window as Tom crawled into the front passenger seat. It was the familiar northern European terrain: muddy fields, the occasional roaming herd of cattle, silos stretching up into the sky. Rural Belgium. Tom relaxed, at least as much as he could. Unconsciously his hand fell to his waistband, where a pistol lay hidden. They would be prepared now if a car pulled up alongside them.

"You're going to be in deep when you get back," Tom said mildly. "I wish I could take the fall for you."

Henrik shrugged. "They'll punish me. But they have to love me for the prestige I'll be bringing them. Oliver Moore, in custody. It's for the greater good, is it not?"

Tom nodded. Henrik had called Interpol for reinforcements. Naturally Interpol would oblige. No doubt agents were being dispatched at this very moment. But Henrik would be in up to his eyeballs for bending rules and using the agency's resources to track Loki's accounts illegally, without waiting to go through the proper channels. It was a risk, yes. On the other hand, if it paid off. . . .

"Did you ever know my brother?" Tom wondered aloud. "Before he turned?"

"Not personally, no." Henrik brushed a tuft of white-gold hair back behind his glasses. "Of course George spoke of him back in those days. Who didn't? His reputation preceded him. Tell me, why is it that the most brilliant agents always lose their way?"

It was a rhetorical question. Tom didn't have to reply. And it wasn't worth thinking about, anyway. Because every agent, no matter how decent or well-intentioned, had once considered taking that same dark fork in the road, the one that had led Loki astray.

Tom included. After all, Loki was his twin. If the seeds of evil could be sown in Loki, then certainly they could be sown in Tom as well.

"How did you first meet George?" Tom asked, eager to change the subject. "He never told me the specifics."

"When I started, I was a commando. . . . Oh, was it twenty years ago already?" Henrik chuckled and shook his head. He glanced in the rearview mirror, then shifted lanes. "George had a mission in Belgium. I helped him on the case. Of course, I was very young then. I made some big mistakes, despite being on such an elite force. Overconfidence, I suppose. I probably hurt more than helped him. But he taught me along the way and saved my life more than once while he was at it."

Tom nodded slowly. "He's a good man," he said quietly, picturing Gaia at George's brownstone. The thought comforted him, if only a little.

"Yes, he is. It's too bad about his wife." Henrik sighed. "But you know, that Katia, I never trusted her."

Tom stiffened. "That Katia?" he repeated.

"Yes," Henrik replied evenly. "I met her several times here in Europe. A beautiful redhead, but she never would look me in the eye. Looking back, it seems obvious now that he was set up."

"Doesn't it," Tom replied, and his body went cold.

GOOD FOOD WAS JUST ONE OF THE

many sweet perks of living with the Mosses. Gaia's eyes widened as she surveyed the spread Olga had laid out for dinner: roast leg of lamb with rosemary, golden new potatoes, glazed carrots, fresh snap peas, a beet salad (Olga's Eastern European touch)—and to top it all off, Olga's special gravy. Olga's gravy was pure genius. A monument to poor health. It was thick and rich and so buttery, it could probably glue arterial walls to each other. Which meant, of course, that it was right up Gaia's alley.

"Wow," Ed said.

Gaia shot him a quick smile from across the table.

"It's such a lovely treat to have a guest," Mrs. Moss announced graciously.

"It's nice to be here," Ed said simply. He raised his eyebrows and flashed a crooked grin. "Thanks for having me."

Mrs. Moss was beaming.

Turn on the charm there, Fargo, Gaia thought, resisting the urge to smirk. She couldn't get over how Ed had dressed up for the occasion—in a crisp white button-down shirt and a pair of new corduroys. Any doubts she'd had about inviting Ed to dinner had evaporated the moment he'd walked through the door.

Gaia still wasn't sure what had possessed her to send that e-mail. True, Mrs. Moss had complained yesterday that the dinner table would be so empty, what with Brendan at the dorm and Paul out with a friend and Mr. Moss away on business—so a part of Gaia had obviously been responding to that. The word *empty* wasn't a word that anybody needed to hear in this place. But a different part of her wanted to test something. That part wanted to see if an unusual set of circumstances—like a semiformal dinner in the presence of an adult—could give her relationship with Ed the kick in the butt it needed to get back to normal. For good.

"Can we start?" Gaia asked.

Mrs. Moss laughed. She draped her napkin across her lap. "Of course, dear."

Once again Gaia felt a strange flush of warmth. That had been happening a lot this evening. *Dear.* It was such a small, incidental snippet of speech. Virtually meaningless. And certainly unconscious on the part of Mrs. Moss. But that was why it elicited such a strong emotion. Mrs. Moss wasn't faking anything for Gaia's benefit. Gaia *was* her "dear." And Gaia knew that she'd brought something into Mrs. Moss's life as well—into the lives of all the members of the Moss family. She brought companionship. It wasn't a one-way street. It was a *real* relationship. Which meant that it was unlike any other she'd experienced in the recent past—except, of course, with Ed.

"It. . . um, helps to chew before you swallow," Ed teased as Gaia shoved a forkful of lamb into her mouth and wolfed it down.

"Very funny," Gaia muttered. She sliced off another chunk of meat.

Ed shrugged at Mrs. Moss. "I apologize for my friend's manners," he said dryly.

Mrs. Moss laughed. Her eyes flashed between the two of them as she served herself some potatoes. "Well, I can certainly see that you fit well together," she remarked. "How long have you been dating?"

Dating?

Stop. Rewind. Delete. Empty recycle bin. Blood surged to Gaia's face, and she found herself cringing. She stared at her plate as if it would somehow magically deliver her from this awful, awkward, miserable moment. . . . Was Ed looking at her? And how could Mrs. Moss not know about Sam? Sam was Brendan's *roommate*. This was mortifying. Gaia could feel him next to her, jiggling his knee, obviously about as relaxed as she was.

"Um. . . we're just friends," Ed mumbled.

Bury me, please. Earthquake. Building collapse. Whatever. Gaia nodded quickly, forcing herself to relax. She glanced up at Ed. His face was the color of the beet salad. He started shoveling food into his mouth.

"Oh, I'm sorry," Mrs. Moss apologized. "I didn't mean to make you uncomfortable."

"No problem," Gaia said. Right. It was no big deal. Mrs. Moss had made a natural mistake. Yet somehow it seemed to resurrect that invisible but very palpable weirdness between Gaia and Ed. Her cheeks were still burning.

Well. She would just have to eat her way through this. Soon enough, the moment would dissipate, maybe five bites from now. Besides, was it really so bad? It was a `normal, painful, family-style moment.` In a way, it was almost as if Mrs. Moss was her own mother—doing what mothers did. Being totally unsubtle.

Gaia paused, fork suspended.

My own mother.

Somehow, despite all the tension and awkwardness, everything became clear to her in that instant. She was in no hurry. She needed to take her time. Oliver was too much of a risk right now. Of course he was. Maybe in a month she'd be ready to join him. But for the present she was happy here. Phenomenally embarrassed, but happy. And hey, Mrs. Moss got something out of the deal, too. She got to make Gaia blush. Call her "dear." Feed her. And most important, she got to enjoy a part of Mary's life, to keep that part of her life alive.

She was Gaia's family now.

SAM'S EYES FLICKERED IN TIME

with the epileptic strobe light behind his eyelids. *On-off, on-off, on-off. . . .*

Bird Man

Was this the white light people talked about when they passed over from life to death? The tunnel to heaven? It didn't seem right. There was nothing comforting about it. Sam didn't feel like he was "coming home," the way people described near-death experiences on those cheap cable shows. So maybe this was the tunnel to hell. Of course. Where else would Sam Moon be headed? His body was gone; he couldn't feel it, couldn't feel anything. Only the searing *on-off, on-off. . . .*

His eyes fluttered open, and a face appeared. It was the handsome face of a man in his late forties. An oddly familiar face. God? *Man. . . made in his own image. . . .* Disjointed phrases from the Bible filtered through Sam's consciousness as he stared up into two bright eyes. Sam had never been a religious guy, but—

"Don't be afraid of me, Sam Moon."

Sam jerked. He tried to bolt upright but couldn't. He *knew* this face somehow—and it was not the face of God. It was the face of a hawk, some kind of giant bird of prey. Yes. His arms felt like granite cylinders at his sides, lifeless, useless. He blinked. The man clicked off the beam of a penlight and tucked it into the breast pocket of a dark suit.

"Glad you finally decided to join us, Sam," the man said. "I was worried our friend had put too much anesthetic in that dart. Quite a sleep you had there, my friend. When we gave you your insulin injection earlier, you barely flinched."

The words flowed together. Sam could understand them, but they were fuzzy, seamless. He fought to make sense of his surroundings. He was strapped to a table in some kind of vast, unfurnished room. Everything was white. "Who are you?" he muttered. "I know you?" His disembodied voice floated up and away from him. It came from far away; it came from underwater.

The man smiled. His eyes were very sharp. Bird eyes. They seemed brighter even than the light that had streamed into Sam's pupils, the light that had resurrected him from his temporary death.

"I am Gaia's uncle, Oliver," the man said. "I do not believe we have met in any formal sense, Sam, but I know who you are. I brought you here."

"Brought me here?" Sam croaked. He was still groggy, but his heart stirred into faster beats now. He was having trouble breathing. "But Josh—"

"He's gone," Oliver reassured Sam in a calm, soothing voice. "You aren't in any danger. Forgive the use of force, but I needed to talk to you alone."

Gaia's uncle. . . .

Sam swallowed. There was a stone in his throat. No, a bowling ball; that was it, a bowling ball—and this bird man was saying something to him now, about how much he loved Gaia, how much he wanted her to go live with him. . . . Sam's thoughts sharpened. The words crystallized into individual shards of a greater whole. And all at once, with terrible, sudden clarity, he understood.

He recognized this voice.

Yes. It was the voice of his worst nightmares. The voice he could never forget. Sam clenched his fists, trying to stop himself from giving in to the nausea rising in his throat, the bilious black sludge threatening to choke him.

"I love her very much," the voice continued. It was smooth and musical, reverberating through the room, through the chambers of Sam's head, where they metamorphosed into other words. . . .

"Cat got your tongue?"

"Do you love her, Sam?"

They were the questions that had haunted Sam night after feverish night, posed by the stranger who had captured him all those months ago—the stranger who had tortured him, the stranger who had denied him the insulin he needed as a diabetic, the stranger who had almost killed him.

But not a stranger. *This* man.

Gaia's uncle.

Oliver (if that was even his real name) smiled cordially at Sam now, offering him water, food, *anything you need.* He was the man at the source, the man who orchestrated. . . . The nausea receded, and an icy coldness gripped Sam's stomach. He was still disoriented, but one thing was clear: he needed to get as far away from this man as possible, as fast as he could. But escape was out of the question. There was no point in even trying.

"I need your help, Sam," the man finished.

Panic fluttered like a wing inside Sam's tight chest. But he forced himself to nod. It was best not to fight. It was best to pretend for as long as possible. Because this was a very dangerous man. Sam knew that. It was a blood memory hard-wired into his veins.

This man was a killer.

"I DIDN'T REALIZE YOU KNEW

Slippery Wheel

Katia so well," Tom said. His eyes bored into Henrik's profile. Only years of rigorous training kept his hands still, his voice calm. Inside, he was a seething mass of confusion and rage. Because Loki had won yet another battle. He didn't even have to be in the same part of the world, but he'd cleverly persuaded Tom to trust this man.

"Loki can really find them," Henrik mumbled, changing lanes.

"I know," Tom breathed. He wasn't lying. Loki had found *him*, after all—this "Henrik," whoever he was. He was certainly not George Niven's old comrade, Special Agent Henrik van de Meulen. No, the real Henrik was no doubt a corpse by now. Tom studied the man's face. The plastic surgery was pretty damn impressive. So was the coaching. But not quite good enough. Because this impostor, good as he was, had gotten his wires—rather, wives—fatally crossed. He'd substituted Katia for Ella. He'd confused the recent death of one with the long-past death of the other. And sealed his own demise in the process.

"We'll meet with Loki soon enough," Henrik said. "We'll take our revenge. For George's sake. And yours."

Tom nodded. "Yes, we will." His voice was as still as a pond. He glanced out of the window, his mind racing. The little car chugged along, past the same drab scenery—with the sun a fiery red ball to their left. *To my left? At sunrise?*

All at once Tom realized that they weren't headed for Amsterdam at all. They were headed southeast, in the wrong direction. And that was the motivation he needed. He had to get control of this car and dispose of Henrik. Now. With a barely perceptible motion, he fished his pistol from his waistband—and in less than a tenth of a second had the barrel shoved against the man's temple.

Henrik flinched slightly, but he didn't turn his head. His gaze remained pinned to the highway.

"Pull over," Tom commanded.

"It's too late, Enigma," Henrik whispered.

"Not if I shoot you," Tom said through gritted teeth. "You pull over now, or you'll be roadkill. I can grab the wheel and pull over myself."

For a few seconds Henrik kept driving, seeming to weigh his options. His knuckles were white on the wheel. But finally he slowed the car and pulled off to the side, over a little grassy knoll and then down a steep embankment to a field. The car lurched to a stop. Tom's gun never wavered, not even for an instant. The barrel remained firmly planted against the impersonator's temple.

"Get out," Tom croaked.

"You should give it up," the man said neutrally. His voice had changed. His consonants were now thick as gravel. "You have no chance of escape, regardless of what you do with me. Loki knows where you are."

Russian. Tom placed the man's accent. This "Henrik" was a Russian, not Belgian-Dutch at all. But as Tom processed this information, tried to make sense of it, something darted at the corner of his peripheral vision. Henrik was reaching for his own weapon. Tom didn't hesitate. He pulled the trigger. It was all over very quickly. There was a muzzle flash, a deafening crack, a painful recoil. Tom winced. His ears rang. Blood spurted from his enemy's skull, splashing onto Tom's shirt. The man flopped against the driver's side window. He was dead.

"Stupid," Tom hissed out loud.

But he wasn't talking to Henrik or whoever the hell he was. He was talking to himself. He'd killed Henrik before he could get any real information out of him. And then he realized something else: That assassin back at the Pension Arboire. . . that hadn't been the Wolf at all. That had been one of Tom's own—a member of the CIA or perhaps Interpol—coming to save him. And this phony Henrik had disposed of that agent before he'd even had a chance to open his mouth.

Tom's heart picked up a beat. He stared at the crimson ooze dripping from Henrik's cranium. Why had Henrik reached for his gun? Perhaps because he knew he was dead, anyway? Yes. Even if he didn't reveal any information, he'd been compromised. Tom had exposed him. Loki would never have allowed him to live.

Move!

The voice came from nowhere. His brain in a fog, Tom went through the motions of dragging Henrik's body from the driver's seat and dumping it in a cesspool by the foot of the slope. Then he returned to the car, started the engine, and sped across the field until he reached a small road, far from the highway.

He knew where he was headed. To the van de Meulen apartment, as he knew it. The sun was his guide. But for some reason, he was having a hard time maintaining his grip on the wheel.

It was only after he'd driven three miles that he realized why. His hands were soaked with blood.

I remember coming to Belgium
with Katia. When was it? Must
have been fifteen years ago. We
left Gaia with her grandmother
and spent a week in Bruges, just
the two of us. They call Bruges
the "Venice of the North." It
was the most romantic week of my
life. We rented a private boat
and spent days drifting up and
down the misty canals, stopping
only for a glass of wine or to
peep into an art museum, inhal-
ing the timeless magic of the
place and savoring the rarity of
being alone together—just the
two of us.

I could never bring myself to
return there. Not since I lost
her. The thought has crossed my
mind many times in recent days,
but I can't afford grief right
now. I need to stay on top of
my emotions. When this thing
with Loki is finished, I'll
take Gaia to Bruges. She would
love it there: the Gothic
churches, the Benedictine

convents peeking through the
fog. It's dark and mysterious,
but somehow warm and welcoming,
too. Like Gaia herself.

   I know I'm presuming too much
to imagine that Gaia would want
to go anywhere with me again. But
I've got to keep assuming that
when the time is right, she'll
let me back into her heart.
She'll understand why I've had to
leave her, and she'll forgive me
for it. Because without Gaia, I
have nothing. I lost everything
else a long, long time ago.

Tom cocked the
hammer. He
thrust the
barrel of the
pistol into
indifference
the fleshy
part of the
neck at the
base of her
skull.

HEATHER SUPPOSED THAT IT WAS

Cocktail Hour

a bit naive to expect Sam to call her back. She hadn't seen him or spoken to him in weeks. For all she knew, he and Gaia had eloped. Maybe he hadn't picked up his messages. Or maybe he had finals. Or had been bitten by a West Nile mosquito and gotten shipped off to the Center for Tropical Diseases in Atlanta or wherever it was.

Yes, life was full of possibilities. Wasn't it wonderful?

A tear spilled onto Heather's mattress as she stared at her phone. She couldn't seem to get out of bed. Maybe she should go to the living room and join her mom. But no, that would be much worse. Her mother was having some women over for cocktails today. Returning full steam to New York society. *Go, Mom.* What bliss at the Gannis home.

"Oh, Heather, dear!" her mom called over muffled peals of laughter. "You sure you don't want to join us?"

"No, thanks, Mom!"

Heather heard her own voice. There wasn't even a trace of sadness, though she'd been crying only seconds earlier. Amazing. Was she as bad as her mother? Was she that capable of deception? Were appearances all that mattered?

No.

Without pausing to second-guess herself, she

grabbed the phone and savagely punched in Ed's number. Her breath came in tight gasps. There was a ring on the other end, that dull buzz. Another. Then a third. He still hadn't responded to her letter, but maybe that was because—

"Hello?" Ed answered.

Heather bit her lip. He sounded so open, so friendly. A wave of hope expanded in her chest.

"Hi," she whispered, her voice choked with longing.

"Heather?" Ed asked.

"Yes."

"Oh. Hi." Ed's voice was toneless. Not mean, not hard. Not much of anything.

"Hi, Ed," Heather whispered, straightening, wondering if her mascara was streaked, if she looked as bad as she felt, but then remembering that he couldn't see her—

"I got your letter. Thanks. But I don't think we should talk more about it right now."

Heather blinked. "You don't?" Her voice faltered.

"No. I've got too much on my mind. I'm. . . I'm sorry."

Heather nodded. In his voice she heard a cacophony of feelings. She heard pain. She heard loss. She heard anger. A lot of things. Or did she?

"I'll talk to you later," he said.

Please feel something, Ed, she pleaded silently, desperately. Indifference was the one thing she couldn't handle. It didn't match his personality. That first "hello" carried such promise. Ed must know how much she loved him. That they could truly start over. That her secret had destroyed their relationship only because it had eaten away at her, turned her into a monster, made her sabotage the one good, real thing in her life. But she had learned, and now—

"Heather?" Ed said softly. "I'll see ya later, okay?"

"Okay."

"Bye."

There was a click, and the line went dead.

Heather's body felt as light and empty as a crumpled paper bag. She squeezed her eyes shut and willed herself not to cry. It didn't work. She sniffed.

Cocktail hour with Mom was sounding better and better.

AS QUIETLY AS POSSIBLE, TOM

Very Russian Eyes

slid Henrik's key into the lock. The door clicked open. He entered the apartment, squinting through the morning sunshine that streamed through the windows. Brightly lit motes of dust danced in the empty foyer.

Where are you, Charlotte?

Classical music floated to him from somewhere deep inside the residence. Tom listened. Bartók. He followed the sound, walking noiselessly into the kitchen. Unwashed dishes sat in the sink, but there was no sign of her. He drifted into a long corridor, and the music grew louder. It was coming from a room at the end of the hall. The door was open just a crack. Tom withdrew his gun and moved toward the music, his back to the wall. Surprise was his best weapon. He held his breath and peered through the doorway.

There she was, busily downloading files off a computer. A Colt .45 with a silencer lay on the desk beside her. Funny. Tom had always found it interesting (and mildly amusing) that foreign terrorists—particularly Eastern Europeans and Russians—seemed to prefer big, bulky, American guns. He had a few theories as to why. Most of them had grown up in repressed societies, under the watchful eye of a secret police. Such gaudy weapons probably made them feel free, as if they were expressing their individuality. Like cowboys. Or cowgirls, in this instance.

Something else struck Tom, too. Aside from the gun, Charlotte could still pass for a perfect housewife. Her blond hair was pulled back in a messy bun. She might have been downloading recipes. Unlikely, though.

Without making a sound, he slid through the doorway

and crept up behind her. Her fingers clicked away on the keyboard. She was oblivious to his presence.

"Good morning," he whispered in Russian.

She lunged for her gun, then froze. Tom's pistol was at her head.

"How nice to see you again, Mrs. van de Meulen," he hissed into her ear.

He spun her desk chair so that she faced him. She regarded him impassively. If any emotion could be said to register in her face, it was disdain. Tom stared hard into her eyes. Now he finally understood why Charlotte had reminded him so much of Katia. It wasn't her smile, her long neck, or her sweet nature. It was her eyes. Those wide-set, almond-shaped, very Russian eyes. She was no Belgian. Tom would bet money that this woman came from a long line of Tartars.

"You're good at masking your accent," Tom said finally. "I really believed you were just a nice Flemish lady."

"Congratulations, I suppose," the woman replied in flawless English.

Tom gestured with the gun for her to stand. The woman obeyed, but she lifted her chin in defiance, her eyes blazing. He jammed the pistol against her head and seized her in a choke hold, then pulled her roughly from the desk—searching for twine, duct tape, anything to keep her still.

"What do you want?" she gasped.

"Open the drawers," he commanded.

She did his bidding even as he held her, pulling out desk drawers and opening cabinets until Tom finally found a ball of tape. It wasn't very strong, but it would do for now. He threw her to the ground and dug his foot into the small of her back. With his free hand he deftly wound the tape around her wrists, biting off the end of it to seal the makeshift set of handcuffs. The acrid taste of glue filled his mouth. He stood, his foot still firmly planted next to her spine.

"Talk," he commanded. "What's the plan?"

She said nothing.

Tom leaned over and smacked her with his pistol—very sharply, in the face.

She flinched but didn't cry out. She was strong, this one. But of course she was. She worked for Loki. Her cheek reddened, and her eyes watered.

"I will not hesitate to kill you, believe me," Tom whispered. "That you're a woman makes no difference. I'll put a bullet in your skull without a second thought."

"Do you think Loki would actually tell *us* the plan?" she grunted in Russian.

"Enough of it, yes."

"Is Sasha dead?" she asked.

Tom frowned. "Sasha?"

"My partner." She groaned. "Henrik."

"He is. And you will be joining him soon."

"Fine. I'm not telling you anything."

Tom cocked the hammer. He thrust the barrel of the pistol into the fleshy part of the neck at the base of her skull. "Your choice," he said.

"Wha—what do you want?" she stammered, squirming.

"The information you gave me," Tom growled. "This physicist in Chechnya. True or false?"

"All of it false," she panted. She tried to squirm again, but Tom kicked her spine. She cringed, then went limp. "Our orders were to stall you," she gasped. "Until we could plan to get you to—"

"Where was Sasha taking me today?" Tom demanded.

"To a private airstrip where a chartered airplane was waiting. You were to fly to the United States."

Tom took a deep breath. So. Everything he'd been told was a fabrication. Chechnya. The trace on Loki's bank account. Everything. This trip to the United States was probably a lie, too. They'd strung him along. Wasted his time.

Or maybe not. At least now he was in a position of power, however fleeting.

"What is my brother's plan?" Tom repeated.

The woman struggled to turn her head. Her blood-shot eyes met Tom's. "If you're going to kill me, do it," she choked out. "Otherwise get out of here!"

It became clear to him then: She was far more

terrified of his twin than she was of Tom—even though Tom was here, pointing a gun at her. But he could use that terror to his advantage. Appearances went a long way. This woman feared him because he was a replica of his brother. He could play that hand. But he had to act quickly.

His eyes flashed to the computer. On the screen was a long list of aliases, most of which Tom recognized: renowned assassins, terrorists. He smacked the woman one last time with the pistol, then snatched the mouse and scrolled down the menu bar. Loki had actually given these scum ID and PIN numbers. And titles as well.

The Wolf (TW): 078654, Project Manager. . . Bernard Ferry (BFF): 884742, Arms Supplier. . . Josh Kendall (J): 666854, Security. . . Sasha Ilyavich (S): 226727, Security . . .

Tom clicked the mouse twice more, shifting to another list. These names he didn't recognize, but their titles turned his blood to ice.

Genetic Consultant. . . Biochemical Engineer . . .

So maybe that anthrax factory in the Sudan wasn't so far off the mark after all. Loki was gathering terrorists and corrupt scientists for some kind of biological weapons project—

DNA.

As the letters sprang from his memory, he shuddered. His informant had mentioned DNA. And Gaia. And kidnapping. His mouth suddenly felt very dry.

His thoughts kept racing, but only down blind alleys. What on earth did any of this have to do with Gaia? None of the pieces of the puzzle seemed to fit.

He turned to the woman on the floor, his gun still trained on the back of her skull.

"I'll ask you again," he said. This time he didn't sound urgent or anxious. Instead he affected an imitation of Loki's own silky tone. "What is my brother's plan?"

"I. . . I. . . I can't tell you. You have to believe me." Her voice rose to a high-pitched squeal. She was panicking now. "He never—"

"That's fine," Tom interrupted. "I'll just leave you here to die, then." Without another word he jabbed the button to eject the disk in the A drive.

"Kill me!" she pleaded shrilly. "Do it now!"

Tom snatched the disk, shoved it into his pocket, and hurried from the apartment, closing the door behind him. Killing her at this point would be an act of mercy. He wasn't in a particularly merciful mood.

"GAIA'S FATHER, AS YOU MUST

Vermin

know, is a very uncaring parent," Oliver stated. He shook his head as if with regret. "He's also a very dangerous man. We aren't certain of the depth of his operation."

Sam swallowed. His flesh crawled. These little touches of sincerity were too much to handle. He nodded and tried to look less than wholly terrified. It took every ounce of effort he could muster. Even though Oliver had unstrapped him and allowed him to sit back on a comfortable leather couch, even though Oliver had fed him a plate of some delicious pasta with cream sauce and red wine—yes, *wine*, no less—Sam was much more frightened now than he was when he'd first emerged from unconsciousness. This place, this loft. . . it was so *huge*. But it was so sparse, too. So cold. Was it a residence? An office? Both? Or was it simply an elegant torture chamber?

"Do you have any questions?" Oliver asked.

Sam shook his head. Oliver seemed very comfortable in his new role as the perfect host. Mr. Congeniality. He almost reminded Sam of Josh—what with that plastic smile and those chiseled good looks. But of course he did. He was toying with Sam, trying to get him to lower his guard. Just as Josh had. Fortunately, Sam had learned his lesson.

"You don't want to know who my employers are?" Oliver pressed.

"Why would I care?" Sam forced himself to reply. The truth was, though, he doubted very much that Oliver had any employers. Everything about him—his dress, his mannerisms, the way he'd treated the burly man who'd brought Sam his food and promptly disappeared into a back room—suggested that *he* was the one who did the employing. *He* was the boss. *He* was the one who'd hired Josh to turn Sam's life into the living death, the purgatory-en-route-to-hell it had long since become.

Oliver smiled. "I work for the government, Sam. So does your friend Josh."

In spite of his horror and fear Sam couldn't help but smile in return. Now, *that* was funny. "You honestly expect me to believe that?" he asked in a tight voice.

"Yes. I do."

It was an interesting approach, Sam had to admit. Maybe Oliver thought that if he presented Sam with the most outrageous, far-fetched scenario, then Sam would be inclined to believe it: reverse psychology taken to the extreme. Or maybe he thought that Sam was an amnesiac. Or maybe he believed his own words. Yeah, that was a distinct possibility, too. Sam had no possible frame of reference with which to judge this man or his actions. Maybe Oliver wasn't merely a psychopath, but a delusional one at that. Because if Sam were to believe that Josh Kendall worked for the CIA, then he might as well believe that Charles Manson had worked for Save the Children.

"Let me just get this straight," Sam said in the silence.

"The government forces people to break the law, and threatens them with laser gun sights, and *kills*—"

"Sometimes we have to push the envelope," Oliver murmured, shaking his head again. "I wish we didn't. But when we are faced with an enemy like Gaia's father, we have no choice. The word *sinister* doesn't even come close to describe his dealings."

Sam stared at him. "He sounds a lot like you," he said.

Oliver chuckled. "He is like me, I suppose. But somewhere along the way he took a different path."

Enough. "What do you want from me?" Sam spat. His patience was nonexistent at this point. He knew that he was here for a reason and that he had two choices: do this guy's bidding or die. The latter was preferable. He just didn't want it to be painful. Another dart in the back would be just fine.

"I want you to bring Gaia to me," Oliver said pleasantly.

Sam shrugged. "That's impossible."

"Why?" Oliver asked, but his tone remained soft, as if they were simply discussing something as banal as meeting for lunch.

"She hates my guts. She doesn't want anything to do with me."

Oliver smiled. "She doesn't hate you, Sam. She loves you. But she's *angry* with you. All she wants from you is to make one last attempt at reconciliation.

That's all I want from you, too. I want all of us to be happy. But this has to be *her* choice. You understand that, don't you?"

Sam didn't answer. He had a vivid hallucination of leaping from the couch and strangling Oliver with his bare hands. But he didn't move a muscle. It wasn't so much the lies that enraged him—it was the knowledge that there was no way out of this. Oliver was truly a genius. He was like a conductor, masterfully orchestrating the symphony of Sam and Gaia's failed relationship. He'd split them apart just so he could bring them back together for his own vile purposes. Whatever they were.

"She'll talk to you," Oliver continued. "Gaia loves you. Trust me."

Trust. That was the word that melted Sam's facade. He couldn't hide the fury in his eyes. He felt clammy perspiration on his palms, in beads on his back. He knew he was only glimpsing the tiniest fraction of Oliver's depravity. The man's face glinted every time he said Gaia's name. *What does he want with her?* Sam shifted in his seat, certain that he had no choice but to play along with this empty charade. For now. As long as he could stay alive long enough to warn Gaia, then—

"I have a cell phone," Oliver murmured. "You can make the call from here."

"Yeah, um—okay," Sam stammered.

Suddenly Oliver's birdlike eyes hardened. "You're lying," he stated in a flat voice. "You don't intend to help at all. I'll have to dispose of you now and convince Gaia of the truth myself."

Panic seized Sam. *No! He's going to kill her!* He shook his head. "N-No, I do. I'm just. . . confused. I—"

"Do you really think you're better than me?" Oliver snapped. "You slept with a married woman twice your age. You helped a known terrorist escape from prison so that you could avoid a murder charge. Don't pretend that you stand on some sort of moral high ground, Sam Moon. You're vermin."

Sam couldn't respond. He could only gape at this man, this bottomless well of agony. The white room went black. Shame and guilt and self-hatred flooded through Sam until there was nothing left but a void. He couldn't take this anymore.

Oliver was right.

Yes, everything he'd said was true. Sam slumped back against the cushions. He wanted to cry, but he couldn't. He didn't have the energy. He had nothing. Nothing but pain.

Oliver's face softened. "You can redeem yourself, though."

Oh God. Sam put his head in his hands. He was quivering, out of control. He couldn't think straight. He only wanted to be delivered. He *did* want to be redeemed. No matter what it took.

"Sam?"

He lifted his gaze.

Oliver pulled a slender cell phone from his suit pocket and held it out to Sam. In Sam's hazy, uncertain state it looked almost like a peace offering, a palm leaf.

"Make the call," Oliver urged.

Sam hesitated. If he made the call, then he would have one last chance to warn Gaia. One last chance to save her—and himself in the process. So he nodded.

Only then did the tears begin to flow.

"Okay," he wept. "Okay."

Here's a profound question: Why do people send around spam e-mails?

More specifically, why do people forward you those stupid spam e-mails in an effort to cheer you up when all they do is piss you off?

Today I got an e-mail (from some meathead at school I don't even know) about some person who had no arms or legs and yet still managed to paint landscapes onto teacups. Yesterday I got one about a woman who bought herself a beautiful dress but kept waiting for a special occasion to wear it, then got run over by a bus. Needless to say, that special occasion never arose.

These messages don't touch my heart or make me think profound thoughts. They make me want to barf. For starters, half of them are made up. Also, they always end with random clichés like "live each day to the fullest" and "be grateful for your health." Does that compel me to thank God that I have all four limbs or vow not to save my dresses (as if I even own any beautiful ones) for special occasions?

Actually, they do compel me to do something. They compel me to send one out on my own. It would go like this:

Once upon a time there was a girl with four limbs (limbs that were hideous and bulging with muscles), a slightly surly disposition, and a penchant for kicking the asses of scumbags. Her mother was murdered. Her father abandoned her. Twice. Her uncle was just plain weird. Still, she survived. She even fell in love. Her boyfriend seemed like a great guy, but it turned out that he had multiple personality disorder. She never once sent him a spam e-mail. In fact, she recently sent him a conciliatory e-mail of sorts,

to which he failed to respond.
*   The End*
*   P.S. If you don't forward this*
to at least twenty people, I will
find you and kick your ass.

Okay, maybe there would be
another postscript, too. It would
not, however, consist of an
inspirational homily. It would be
a reality check. Something along
the lines of how misfortune, misery, and loneliness are the guid-
ing forces of the universe. The
world is a freaky, hard-core
place. Bad things happen to people who don't deserve it. All the
time.

Oh, yeah—and here's the
kicker. You know that old saying:
"What doesn't kill you makes you
stronger"? Well, that's a lie.
What doesn't kill you definitely
doesn't make you stronger. What
doesn't kill you hurts a lot and
scars you for life.

That's my final message.

Women. Can't live with 'em. Can't live without 'em.

Why do clichés get such a bad rap, anyway? They're *true,* aren't they? Otherwise they wouldn't have become clichés in the first place.

Not that Gaia Moore is just any woman. But I'm trying to figure out why she blew off our lunch date. We were all set for meatball heroes. She *likes* meatball heroes. Besides, it's not like her to stand me up. Okay, okay—I know I'm contradicting myself. The fact is, I don't know what's "like" her and what's not "like" her anymore. But I thought things were improving. Wrong again. The old emotional barometer is clearly still dipping and diving. One minute she's desperate to hang with me, the next she ditches me.

Then again, lunch is hardly a priority when your whole world has gone to pieces.

I know I should be mad at her.

In fact, it kind of makes me mad
that I'm *not* mad at her. But
somehow, even when Gaia screws
up, I don't feel put off. I just
want to help. I want to volunteer
for the Gaia Moore disaster
relief initiative.

And why is it that when you're
desperate to help somebody, somebody *else* is always desperate for
help that they really don't need?
That somebody else being a certain Heather Gannis?

Whoops. I'm not going to think
about Heather anymore. Right.
That's my new resolution. Not
until we can be the same old non-
friends we were before I met
Gaia. After all, you know what
they say. Two's company. Three's
a crowd.

She'd get
her ass
whipped and
go home
feeling even
lower than
she already
did.

an

army

THE AGENCY SAFE HOUSE IN DOWN-

town Brussels dated to just after the World War II—a nondescript building on a narrow lane, not far from the café where Tom had first met "Henrik." It looked like it hadn't been cleaned or maintained since the fifties. The interior was a ramshackle collage of peeling paint, stained rugs, and chipped fixtures; the stale odor of old cigarette smoke clung to the shadowy walls. But decrepitude was fine with Tom. An intruder would be a lot less likely to suspect that the darkened top floor had been equipped with a state-of-the-art computer system or that a member of the Agency was hiding up here.

Tom rubbed his exhausted eyes and studied the screen once more.

He'd researched the list of names and discovered that Loki had employed a large number of molecular biologists from top biomedical institutes in Europe and the United States. There were other files on the disk as well: a profile of several money launderers, a detailed portfolio of accounts in various banks in the Middle East and South America, and another list of names that Tom didn't recognize—all accompanied by the title *Surrogate*. The word was chilling in its ambiguity.

What's the connection? How are these files linked?

Even after two hours, Tom was no closer to finding any answers.

He clicked the mouse and shifted to the one untitled document on the disk. It was encrypted text, gibberish—except for one word at the top: *CLOFAZE*. His eyes narrowed, and he quickly opened the decoding program. The computer whirred and clicked. An hourglass appeared in place of the mouse icon. Tom leaned back in the chair. This could take some time. He stretched and yawned. His stomach growled. He couldn't remember the last time he'd eaten or slept—

Bingo.

This computer was fast—much faster than he'd expected. The unreadable symbols vanished, instantly replaced by a series of diagrams: segments of the double helix of a DNA strand. The segments began to divide and duplicate themselves. There was no explanatory text, but Tom didn't need any. One word instantly leapt to mind: *cloning.*

He held his breath as the animation abruptly switched to various pie charts, graphs—and finally what appeared to be a kind of tree. Each branch featured one of the names of the people or organizations Tom had seen in the previous files.

He shook his head, frowning. So. All the evidence seemed to indicate Loki was putting together some kind of cloning project. But why? Cloning was hardly a moneymaker. Aside from universities, there weren't that many people in the world willing to pay for a replica of an organism—

Humans.

Of course. Loki didn't intend to clone any organism. He intended to clone a human being. Himself, probably. Yes. Tom almost laughed. This was just the project for a narcissistic sociopath like Loki. Straight out of a B science fiction movie. And it was ironic, in a way, because such a clone already existed. Tom saw him every time he looked in the mirror.

He jiggled his leg, scratched his chin. This didn't make sense. People had been talking about cloning human beings for years and years—first in fiction, then after Dolly the lamb—but the scientific community had always decried it. There were the obvious moral implications, of course, but also, nobody believed that it could be successfully done, at least not for a while. There were too many unknowns. Of course, Loki had always been ambitious. And he'd never lacked hubris.

Maybe this was another decoy.

Tom groaned. He'd been duped *again*. Somehow that woman must have—

The screen suddenly cleared.

The words *Optimal Operative* appeared, accompanied by a faceless, featureless, three-dimensional woman's figure. The figure began to rotate, and a detailed cross section of her brain blinked into a window in the upper-right corner. A magnification process began until a single brain cell filled the small frame. The cell then morphed into a strand of DNA.

The figure froze, instantaneously replaced with a recognizable human being.

Tom stopped breathing.

His insides turned to stone. *No. No.*

He knew then that he hadn't been duped at all. This was no decoy. This was the real thing. The missing piece of the puzzle. And until that moment he had believed he had experienced every possible horror: torture of the most brutal kind, the decimation of entire populations, murder in every conceivable form. . . but in a flash, all those atrocities were somehow made insignificant. Nothing could compare to the blank face that was staring back at him from the screen.

It belonged to Gaia.

Gaia.

Tom gripped the sides of the desk. He was dizzy, listing to one side. The animation resumed. Gaia's figure began to move—to jump, to kick. All the while her face remained flat. Windows opened beside her.

Height: 5'10"
Weight: 145 pounds
IQ: 165
Languages: English, French, Spanish, Italian, Russian, Arabic, some German
Martial arts: kung fu, karate, judo, jujitsu, *muay thai*

This was Gaia's life. It included every vital statistic. Every detail.

A final window opened at the top of the screen.

Greatest asset, Tom read in disbelief. He inhaled sharply as the blinking cursor spelled a single word below it: *Fearlessness.*

"No." This time he whispered the word out loud.

Gaia's figure began to replicate.

The screen divided in half, then into quarters, then into sixteenths—

Tom squeezed his eyes shut. The universe spun and did a nosedive. Loki wanted to mass-produce his own niece. He wanted to replicate everything about her: the physical strength, the cognitive abilities—and most of all, that one fatal flaw: the inability to feel fear. It was beyond evil. There was no word for it. Tom had struggled his entire life to protect Gaia from herself, to make sure that this genetic anomaly could never cause her harm. *That* was why he had taken the time to train her in kung fu, jujitsu, and karate, why he had taken the time to nurture her intellect. He couldn't bear the thought of her putting herself into danger without recognizing its consequences.

Optimal Operative.

Oh, yes. It was all very clear now. The phrase burrowed into Tom's brain, gnawed at his insides. Loki saw fearlessness as a strength. And it was, for an elite fighting force. For an army. An army of Gaias. In a sense, Loki's plan *was* biological warfare, after all. But not the way Tom had envisioned it.

He had to warn her. He had to get back to the States. Nothing else mattered. Anxiety gripped him so tightly that he couldn't move; it strapped him to his chair. He saw everything so clearly in that moment; he'd been so consumed with Gaia's safety that he'd completely neglected it—

The door crashed open.

"Hey!"

Before Tom could turn or even open his eyes, there was a sharp crack at the base of his skull. He saw a flash of white lightning. It was the last thing he remembered.

GAIA WALKED ANOTHER AIMLESS

Solitaire circle around Washington Square Park. What was that? Lap number twelve? Laps weren't working. Nothing was working. She couldn't quiet the dialogue in her head. *Living with Oliver would be the best thing for me. No, it wouldn't. Yes, it would. No, it wouldn't*—Why wasn't there a pill to stop thought? Gaia wasn't one for drugs, but she vowed then and there that if she could find anything to turn off her brain, she would. The worst kind of overthinking was the kind that didn't get you anywhere. And you knew it, but you couldn't help it, anyway. You were just left with an endless replay of the same fruitless questions—ones to which you could never hope to supply the answers.

What fun.

She glanced over to the chess tables. Zolov was finishing off Renny. Funny, she'd seen this same scene a hundred times. Usually it made her smile. Not this afternoon. She felt like she was looking at two people from another lifetime.

Zolov raised his eyes and smiled, somehow sensing her gaze. "Ceendy? You vill play chess today?"

"No." She shook her head. "Not today."

Before either of them could engage her any further, she turned abruptly and trudged away. Why had she even come here? She didn't want to be rude, but chess would only make things worse. She'd get her ass whipped and go home feeling even lower than she already did. No. There was only one way to restore self-esteem today. Kicking someone else's ass. Finding some creep, some wife-beating lowlife or child-raping scuzzbag and helping to introduce their front teeth to the sidewalk.

But Murphy's Law prevailed. It always did, as far as she was concerned. You drop a piece of pizza; it always lands cheese-side down. You look for trouble; Washington Square Park is as peaceful as a nursery.

Out of nowhere a wave of extreme sadness washed over her, so forceful, it almost took her breath away. And with it came a string of mental Polaroids: images of all the times Gaia and Sam had played chess together. All the times they'd sat on the benches. Loafed on the lawns.

The park was the backdrop to their history.

She paused at the Arc de Triomphe and peeked behind her. Zolov and Renny were already back at their game. A few homeless people shuffled down the gravel paths, jostling oblivious NYU students. The air was still, stagnant. The sky was like faded denim. Right now the park looked like some old beat-up set from a movie long over and long forgotten, littered with discarded napkins and empty Snapple bottles.

Gaia shook her head. It was time to get out of here. Find a new park. Some new hangout for all the good times with great new people that lay ahead. Oh, happy day. Maybe it was time to find a new game, too. How about solitaire? Sure. Perfect. She turned her back and kept walking, under the arch and up Fifth Avenue. Yes, she'd just reached an important decision. She picked up her pace. She'd overstayed her welcome. It was time to move on. And maybe she could—

"Leave me the hell alone!"

The shout came from her right, from a little alley tucked in between two historic NYU administration buildings. The voice was female. Somehow, amidst all the traffic and random bits of conversation, Gaia had honed in on the tone, almost unconsciously. There was fear in it. She peered down the narrow passage. A slender African American girl—decked out in bell-bottom jeans, sandals half a foot high, and one of those painfully hip baby T-shirts—was backing away from an older white guy with a beard and a wool hat. He'd practically pinned her against the brick wall.

"I don't want any!" the girl shouted. "How many times do I have to tell you?"

A drug sale.

Gaia's jaw tightened.

Of course. Only a dealer would be brazen (or idiotic) enough to threaten a girl in broad daylight, in such close proximity to so many people. The girl's eyes flashed to the street, briefly connecting with Gaia's own. Judging from the girl's face, she was about Gaia's age, maybe a little older, a college student, no doubt.

She was afraid.

Gaia stormed into the alley. Her luck had changed. She *had* found a lowlife to pummel. Her entire body was an engine, pumping with fiery gasoline. But this wasn't the usual precombat rush. This was pure rage. The scene was too familiar, too much like the first time Gaia had ever met

Mary. . . Mary, trapped in an alley—helpless, alone. Trapped by scum like this guy. For all Gaia knew, this sleazebag might be Skizz's replacement. He probably was, in fact. He was working Skizz's old turf.

"What are you looking at?" the guy demanded.

"Not much," Gaia mumbled under her breath.

He laughed. "Good one. I haven't heard that since the fifth grade."

The girl backed away from him.

"What's going on here?" Gaia asked.

"None of your goddamned business," he shot back.

"Fine."

Gaia's legs were in motion before he saw anything coming. This was a tactic she'd learned from some of the darker passages of the *Go Rin No Sho,* the ancient book of martial arts philosophy her dad had forced her to read all those years ago. It was a cheap shot, at least by the standards of honorable combat—by holding her enemy's gaze, she'd drawn his attention away from the impending kick. Even as she leaped into the air, her limbs a whirl of focused power, she kept staring at him. . . staring and staring until *crack!*—her left foot connected with his temple.

He collapsed to the ground.

"No!" the girl shrieked.

Stunned, Gaia regained her balance. The girl fell at the guy's side. She slapped his pale cheeks, frantically trying to revive him, then shot Gaia a furious glare.

"What did you do *that* for?" she barked.

"I, uh—I thought. . . ." Gaia had no idea what to say. Something was very wrong here. She swallowed, breathing heavily. Blackness hovered at the edges of her vision. She felt faint, the way she always did after battle, but she didn't think she'd exerted herself enough to warrant passing out. That would be all she needed right now.

The guy groaned.

"You thought *what?*" the girl spat. She shook her head and caressed his darkening forehead. "That you'd beat somebody up for kicks? Jesus! You know, I should call the cops." She squinted toward the street. "This is sick. *Sick.*" She seemed to be talking to herself more than Gaia.

"I thought he was trying to sell you drugs," Gaia said, fighting to regain her strength.

"Well, you thought wrong, then, didn't you?"

"But I—"

"It was none of your freaking business what we were talking about."

The guy's eyelids fluttered. "Whasa. . . what's happening?" he moaned.

Best not to answer that, Gaia thought. She tried to smile. "I'm really sorry," she said.

The girl ignored her.

Gaia opened her mouth again, then thought better

of it. She was too weak. She felt like puking. The reality of the situation struck her with the force of one of her own punches: she'd just knocked an innocent guy out cold. And why? But it was best not to answer that, either. She turned and shambled back onto the street. One thing was certain, though: in spite of the fact that she wanted to lie down in the gutter and die, the experience wasn't a total wash. Yes, at the very least she'd proved her own point. It *was* time to move on. Time to get the hell out of this neighborhood for good. Solitaire was sounding better and better.

Sick Fetish

TOM BLINKED AS SOMEBODY'S FACE swam into view. His head was pounding. He was lying on the floor, looking up at. . . *who*? A woman. A woman who was pointing a gun at him. Her features were fuzzy, and for a moment he thought he was hallucinating. His heart squeezed painfully. This one looked even more like Katia than Charlotte had. He couldn't believe it. Maybe this was some kind of sick fetish of Loki's—to find female agents who bore a striking resemblance to Tom's dead wife. Or maybe Loki had them surgically altered. After all, Loki's feelings for Tom's wife were no secret, either.

"Get up," the woman barked, motioning for him to stand.

Careless, Tom thought, angry at himself. No, foolish. He'd been so engrossed with the computer disk, he'd forgotten to take even the most rudimentary precautions. He shook his head and sat up, tapping the back of his skull. His fingers came back wet with blood. But that was a good sign. If the wound hadn't scabbed yet, then he hadn't been out for very long.

He glanced at the computer. She'd turned it off. The disk was no longer in the drive.

"Move it!" she ordered.

Tom nodded absently and lumbered to his feet. He overplayed his wooziness, teetering toward the desk. The woman lowered her gun for a split second, perhaps debating whether or not to steady him. It was just the opportunity he needed. *Now!* He spun, lashing out with his foot, striking a pressure point just above her ankle. She cried out and crumpled slightly. With one hand Tom wrenched the gun away from her and completed the spin, using the momentum to smash his other elbow against her forehead.

She tumbled to the floor, flat on her back.

"Bastard," she spat in Russian. She clutched her skull with both hands.

Tom cocked the hammer and pointed the gun at

the woman's heart. "Tell me where Loki is," he panted, patting her down for the disk. He snatched it from her back pocket and shoved it in his own. His own pain seemed very far away.

The woman remained silent.

"Tell me!" he snapped.

"He's in New York," she muttered finally.

Tom waited.

"Chelsea. That is all I know," she finished. She removed her hands from her face. Her eyes blazed with fury.

"That's it?"

"You can go to hell. You're a dead man."

Tom's fingertip danced over the trigger. He hesitated for a moment. That face prevented him from shooting her; even in a rage, her features reminded him too much of Katia's. But maybe *that* was why Loki chose these women. Because he knew how hard it would be for Tom to harm anyone who resembled his wife.

If you let her live, you'll just be giving him another victory.

He fired the bullet.

From: smoon@alloymail.com
To: gaia13@alloymail.com
Time: 8:05 A.M.
Re: Confused

Hi, Gaia,

    Sorry I didn't reply sooner. I've been busy.

    Thanks for your letter. I'm glad you sent it. I do want to talk. I'm ready to tell you everything. Can you meet me tonight for dinner at the Bubble Lounge on Church Street, 8 P.M.? Please say yes.

                       Sam

Was this a date?
The answer was
most probably no,
even though it had
all the **critical**
trappings of a
date: **juncture**
girl meets boy
alone for dinner
at a fancy Tribeca
restaurant.

"HEY!" ED HELD UP A HAND AND signaled to Gaia as she carried her lunch tray through the cafeteria, right past his table. If it wasn't for those freaking crutches, he'd jump out of his chair and plant himself in front of her. "Earth to Gaia! Over here!"

Right Wrong Time

Finally.

She paused and shot Ed one of her impenetrable stares. Then she smiled. Slightly, anyway. "Oh. I'm sorry," she said. She slid into a chair behind him.

Ed frowned. "Anything you want to tell me?"

She swirled a fork through the slush of yellow-and-white goo that supposedly passed for the Village School cafeteria's mac and cheese. "Not particularly," she said.

Hmmm. At least the blunt honesty was back.

"You ditched me the other day," he said. "One day you're inviting me to dinner at the Mosses' house; the next you're blowing me off. So I'm just trying to figure out if I'm missing anything. If I did something wrong. If maybe you're trying to avoid me."

Gaia shrugged. "Oh, no. It's not that. Sorry."

He laughed bitterly. "That's it? That's the best you can do? Sorry?"

She didn't lift her eyes from her plate.

"Forget it," he muttered. He glared at her. He wanted to take one of his crutches and smash her over the head. No, actually what he wanted to do was stand up and make a speech. It would go like this: *"I love you, Gaia. I love your ratty pants. I love your sour attitude, your mood swings, your crazy life, your surreal past. Your secrets. I love you when you're bitter, angry, out of your mind, happy, nasty. It doesn't matter. I don't care. Just so long as it's you."*

Right. Chances of that happening: about one in eight billion. This was no cheesy teen romance where everything had a happy ending, as if by magic. This was the real world—the world of dog shit on your shoe, lousy school food, horrible accidents, and most of all, rejection.

Gaia shoved a forkful of goo into her mouth.

The inevitable question posed itself again, though: What did he have to lose? So she'd reject him, anyway. So he'd make a huge ass of himself.

So what?

Maybe now was the right time. Precisely because it seemed so wrong. Ed should just throw it out there. Besides, he might spontaneously combust if he didn't. The confession was like hot air in a balloon, pumping him up and up until he was ready to pop. Yes, now—in the cafeteria, between bites of macaroni, with the squeak of chairs and the imbecilic conversation of students—now seemed weirdly appropriate.

"Gaia, there's something I want to tell you," he said quietly. He was surprised by how calm he sounded. He took a deep breath, his heart pounding—then closed his mouth.

Out of the corner of his eye he'd spotted Heather. She was staring at him but quickly looked away. His gaze flicked back to Gaia.

"What?" Gaia prompted.

The moment was gone. The air in the balloon shrank to a comfortable pressure.

"I wanted to tell you that, um. . . I wanted to cash in a rain check on that lunch. Wanna go to dinner tonight?"

Hey, it was a decent save. And maybe it was best to go with candlelight. Yes, that way if he had another momentary bout of insanity and decided to make the confession tonight, he wouldn't be able to see her horrified reaction so clearly.

"Can't," Gaia replied, without looking up. "I'm having dinner with Sam."

"Oh," Ed said. He shrugged and smiled. He felt like he'd just been tossed into a fiery pit and was now slowly roasting to death. But it wasn't so bad. It was a feeling with which he was very familiar. It happened several times a day, usually. "Some other time, then."

"SO YOU'RE SAYING TOM ESCAPED,"

Temper Tantrum

Loki said dryly. He clutched the tiny Nokia cell phone at his ear, strolling aimlessly about the loft. "He never arrived at the airport."

"Sir, I've been waiting here for hours, and they just didn't show," the terrified voice on the other end of the line squeaked. "I can assure you, I've done everything you—"

"Shut up." Loki had a great urge to take the cell phone and smash it against the exposed brick wall of his loft, imagining that it was the skull of this feeble pilot. He had no time to listen to excuses, to sit through the frightened defense of an aborted mission. It wouldn't make a difference, anyway. So instead of smashing the cell phone to smithereens, Loki abruptly clicked off. A temper tantrum wouldn't be of much use at this critical juncture. He needed to focus, to counter his losses, to make some serious adjustments.

Gaia.

Yes. If Tom had indeed escaped, then there was only one place he could be heading. Home to his daughter.

Loki punched in Josh Kendall's cell phone number.

"Yes?" Josh answered in the middle of the first ring.

"I want round-the-clock surveillance of seven-seven-six-two-four-four. Effective immediately."

"But I thought you—"

"You thought?" Loki snapped. "I don't pay you to think. Remember?"

"I—yes. Yes, sir."

"Right," Loki said evenly. "Zero-zero-two is closing in. I want the former subject monitored."

"Yes, sir."

"One more thing. We've discussed the messenger's new role." Loki peered out the giant glass windows that provided him with an uninterrupted view of the Hudson. "Time is truly of the essence now. He must persuade Gaia to come to me by ten P.M. tonight." He paused, watching a cargo ship carving a frothy wake in the river's surface. "And if the messenger doesn't deliver by ten, he must be executed."

There was only the briefest pause before Josh responded.

"Understood," he said.

"DON'T YOU LOOK GORGEOUS," MRS. Moss breathed as she peeked around the door to Mary's bedroom.

Gaia stared doubtfully into the full-length mirror

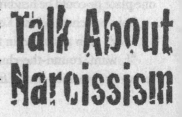

Talk About Narcissism

of Mary's closet. *Gorgeous* was hardly the word that leapt to mind. Yes, she was wearing a dress, plain brown—one she'd bought with Mary, all those months ago. And why, she did not know. Dresses hardly worked wonders for her. All they did was accent her freakishly big muscles. *I look like a man in drag,* she reflected miserably.

"Do you mind if I ask you something?" Mrs. Moss said quietly.

"No, not at all." Gaia turned to her. She felt like adding: *As if you even need to ask.*

"Is this a date?"

Gaia grinned, even though she felt very far from happy at the moment. That was a very good question, in fact. Was this a date? The answer was most probably no, even though it had all the trappings of a date: girl meets boy alone for dinner at a fancy Tribeca restaurant. But the sad truth of the matter was that this was a breakup. An official ritual to end a ruined relationship. An act of closure.

"I'm not sure," she said finally, not wanting to worry or depress Mrs. Moss.

Mrs. Moss smiled back at her. "I know what you mean," she said, her eyes twinkling.

Gaia turned back to the mirror. If only that were true. If only anybody had any idea what *anyone* meant. Right now, everybody in Gaia's life seemed to be speaking a dead language that she had never learned.

Tears started to well in her eyes. *Damn it.* She could see the salty water pooling there, dripping from her lashes. She shook her head, furious for wasting Mrs. Moss's time, furious for losing control in front of her. But of course, Mrs. Moss's features only softened in compassion and sympathy. *She doesn't need your stupid problems,* Gaia cursed herself silently. The woman's daughter had died. And now here was Mary's friend, imposing on Mary's family, crying over a *boy,* of all trivial things. Talk about narcissism.

Mrs. Moss bit her lip. "Gaia, I won't pry if you don't want me to—"

"No, I'm sorry," Gaia interrupted, sniffling. "It's just. . . things are confusing right now. On a lot of different levels."

"I know," Mrs. Moss said quietly. "But remember, if you stick with something long enough, the bumps smooth themselves out in the end. Patience is all it takes. Patience and a little bit of faith."

Gaia laughed grimly. "I don't know if that's true."

"It's true for me, Gaia. For this whole family. That's why we want you to stay here with us."

"What?" The simplicity of the statement caught Gaia off guard. She turned toward the door again and much to her shocked surprise saw that Mrs. Moss's cheeks were damp as well. She really *did* want Gaia to stay. She must have sensed Gaia's hesitancy about her uncle. Or perhaps she'd just grown accustomed to having Gaia around the house. Maybe she didn't want to lose another teenage girl, even one who wasn't her daughter. Whatever the reason, something snapped into place for Gaia at that moment. She felt a kind of inner calm she hadn't felt in weeks.

This is my home.

Yes. The problems were definitely far from over. But in one area of her life she finally had a grip. A tenuous one, maybe, but it was better than falling off the cliff altogether. Gaia's face brightened through her tears. If she could feel centered anywhere, it was here.

Besides, if Oliver was the loving uncle he claimed to be, he could still be in her life. He could visit, hang out with her, whatever. And should her dad suddenly decide to reappear, he could track her down, too. So could George. Gaia was here for the finding. But she knew hands down that living with her biological family didn't work out for her. Which was okay. She was at peace with it. It was okay.

TOM HURRIED THROUGH THE BRITISH

Too Trusting

Airways terminal toward the gate, shaking his head. He'd been forced to take the Concorde. There was going to be hell to pay for the grotesque expenditure. The Agency had a limited budget. His superiors couldn't afford to throw money around, not even when it came to a criminal mastermind like Loki—something for which he'd been reprimanded more than once. But Tom didn't have a choice. The Concorde was due to leave in a little over an hour, and it was the fastest way to get to the United States. The choice was that simple: either shell out the seven thousand dollars on the Agency's tab for a ticket on the Concorde or hijack a fighter jet.

"Coffee or tea, sir?" a uniformed woman inquired as Tom spotted an empty couch near the window. The lounge offered all manner of first-class amenities to its elite group of passengers: free cocktails, finger sandwiches, private movies. "A drink, perhaps?"

"Not for me, thanks." Tom moved quickly to the glass, gazing out into the night to the sleek supersonic jet on the brightly lit tarmac, its needle nose pointing to the black horizon. Anxiety took hold as he lifted his eyes. There were no stars, no moon in sight. A wind howled. Rain began to tick against the windowpane. *Just English weather,* he reassured himself. *Best not to dwell on it.*

He turned back toward the terminal and spotted a bank of public telephones. There was some business that needed attention before he boarded. He picked an isolated booth and dialed a private cell phone number.

George Niven picked up on the first ring.

"Hello?"

"I'm coming home," Tom said. "I need you to pick me up in a few hours."

"Tom," George gasped in relief. "Thank God. I've been trying to reach you. Henrik's number has been disconnected—"

"He's dead," Tom interrupted.

There was silence. "I. . . see," George said slowly. And with that, he recovered himself and moved on— as they always did—to more pressing matters. Explanations and mourning would wait. "There's been a serious development. We've been monitoring Gaia discreetly as you've wanted."

"She's all right?" Tom asked.

"Yes. But we are concerned about her boyfriend. It appears Sam Moon may have helped Oliver escape from prison. There's an investigation pending."

Tom's stomach jackknifed. This was not good news. Clearly Loki was using Gaia's boyfriend to get to her. She wouldn't come of her own free will, so she had to be tricked. No doubt Loki had blackmailed the boy in some horrible way. Gaia was strong and smart, but she could be trusting as well. Too trusting. Tom knew how she felt about Sam Moon. And Tom thought he'd gotten a good feel for Sam's strength of character, too. Of course, once Loki was involved, a person's will and conscience became playthings, toys for him to manipulate.

"Loki is in Chelsea," Tom whispered urgently. "I

don't know where. But under no circumstances may Gaia have contact with Sam Moon. I don't care if you have to blow your cover. Just get her. I'll be in New York in exactly three and a half hours."

"Understood. Be strong, Tom."

Tom swallowed. "You too." He hung up the phone.

For a moment he stood still, rubbing his temples. He was so tired—

There was a crackle of static. He frowned and emerged from the booth. Was that the boarding call already? He wasn't due to depart for another hour.

The PA system leaped to life.

"Attention, all passengers," a nasal female voice announced. "Due to inclement weather, all flights are currently delayed. Please see your ticket agents for further information."

You may not believe this, Tom,
but I'm rather pleased that
you've eluded capture thus far.
I'm certain by now that you've
even discovered my whereabouts.
I'm impressed with your tenacity,
your skill. I welcome it, in
fact. It makes the game between
us a little more challenging.
There is no glory in an easy
victory.

As you well know, I've been
dealing with weaker opponents all
my life. No one else can match me
in terms of mettle and cunning.

True, there is a certain pleasure
in working with a person's mind—
especially a strong one, like the
mind of this college student who

made the mistake of getting too
close to Gaia—and over time,
bending it to meet your needs. Of
playing fear against fear and
betrayal against betrayal until

it is stripped of everything,
until it becomes a vessel to be
filled. Until it can change
other minds. A domino effect of

brainwashing. Although I prefer
to think of it as persuasion.

Especially in Gaia's case.

Sam Moon will persuade her to
come to me. And I will persuade
her of her destiny.

Make no mistake, though. You
cannot stop me from succeeding.
Even in the unlikely event of my
death, my plan will reach its
inevitable conclusion. I've
arranged it that way, for this
operation is far greater than any
one man's life—even my own.

And where does that leave us,
Tom? As you can see, I am not
beyond admiring you. We do share
the same DNA, after all. But you,
Tom, have squandered your natural
gifts, never fully realized your
potential. This makes you a hypo-
crite. A coward. In fact, when
you are stripped of your various
skills and moral posturing, you
are nothing more than a common
thief.

I have never been a thief. A
killer, yes, but never a thief.

But you have stolen from me:
first Katia, then Gaia. You took
what was destined to be mine.

   Thankfully, I can now right
the wrongs of the past.

He saw the
truth in all
of its ugly *new*
simplicity:
he had **hangout**
no power
left over
his own
life.

"GOTTA UPDATE YOU ON A COUPLE

Hidden Chamber

of things, Sammy," Josh announced as he burst into Sam's dorm room. He had the usual grin plastered to his face, but Sam could see effort there. Josh looked frightened. Sam felt a flash of pleasure. If Josh was afraid, then maybe he and Sam were in the same boat. Maybe Josh had failed Oliver in some way. Maybe he was a marked man as well.

"I know what I'm doing," Sam mumbled. He slipped on a rumpled blazer and glanced in the mirror. "I know what to say to Gaia."

That was no lie. Sam planned on telling Gaia everything: what he'd been made to do for Oliver and what Oliver wanted him to do next. He knew he was ensuring his own execution by doing so. But he was at peace with the decision. In fact, he was eerily calm. Maybe he was experiencing the same emotion that condemned prisoners felt on their way to a lethal injection.

"We've got a short time frame here," Josh continued. "You'll be escorting Gaia to her uncle's place by ten tonight."

Sam turned and scowled at him. "Your boss didn't say anything about that. He said that I had to—"

"Change of orders," Josh snapped. The smile

171

vanished, only this time it didn't return. A muscle in his jaw twitched. "You'll be taking her to him tonight. Now repeat back to me what you're going to tell her. I want to hear you say it."

"Some other time. I'm going to be late." He pushed past Josh and headed through the door into the suite's common area.

Josh's hand clamped down on Sam's shoulder— *hard.*

"Not so fast," he growled.

Sam saw red. He spun and drove his fist straight for Josh's face. Josh turned, but not fast enough. Sam's knuckle connected with jawbone, then slid into the wood of the door. An agonizing tingle shot through the bones of his hand, and he recoiled in pain. And then he couldn't breathe. Josh had him in a choke hold. Sam snatched at the door handle with his hand. One of the knuckles was split and oozing a trickle of blood. White spots danced in front of his eyes. But he was going to get out of that dorm room—

"Let him go," a voice commanded behind them.

Abruptly Josh released Sam's neck. Choking for breath, Sam turned and found himself face-to-face with a stocky young man in a black turtleneck and leather jacket. He was brandishing a pistol. His face was scarred, cold.

"Now," the man said blankly. "Let's hear what you're going to say to Gaia."

Sam took a long, deep breath. He couldn't stop staring at the gun. Sooner or later, a bullet was going to find him. But he couldn't dwell on that now. *Just do what they ask and get out of here. It's your only chance.*

"Your uncle loves you," he said mechanically. "He came to talk to me because he knows we're close, and. . . ." He went on and on, but he was no longer even listening to himself. The fabrications were accompanied by a strange sense of dislocation. His lips moved, but his brain had separated from the words. It was as if his inner self—the part of him that was still Sam—had sealed itself off in a chamber no one could find. And in that chamber he saw Gaia. He saw her hands, her lips, her hips. He felt her kiss. The image sent shooting pains through his heart, far more acute than the wounds on his bloodied hand. But there was no use in being morbid, hopeless, defeated. No use in thinking in the past tense. Loki didn't own Sam. Josh didn't own him. Only Gaia owned any part of him at all, and he would keep that part safe and alive until she learned the truth. . . .

"Good enough?" Sam demanded.

Josh looked pensive for a moment. He and the gunman exchanged a glance. Then he shifted into old-style-Josh mode and slapped Sam on the back. "Go get 'em, tiger!" he joked, giving Sam a light push toward the door.

As Sam exited the suite, he felt hollow. But he

couldn't let the emptiness consume him. He had to galvanize his inner optimist. He still had free will. He still had power. The very fact that Oliver needed him so badly was proof of that power. He was a player; he was on the board; they hadn't yet knocked him off.

He could still save Gaia.

But the more Sam told himself these things, the less he believed it. And as he left the dorm, the final shreds of illusion melted away. He saw the truth in all of its ugly simplicity: he had no power left over his own life. Nor any power left over Gaia's. Once he was dead, Gaia was sure to follow. It would only be a matter of time. With each step he took, he drew closer and closer to the end. Like walking the plank.

"WHAT DO YOU MEAN, YOU'RE STILL not sure?" Tom barked at the ticket agent. "Don't you have meteorologists in this country?"

"Sir." The woman offered Tom a pacifying, sympathetic smile that aggravated him even more. "I've told you. We don't

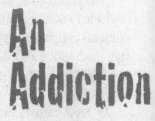

An Addiction

have a departure time for your flight. When we do, I will announce it over the PA system."

"This is ridiculous," Tom growled. "For Christ's sake, this is the Concorde."

The woman's smile remained unchanged, as if it had been simply stamped on her face. "All flights are affected by the weather, sir."

Tom ran his hand through his hair. Maybe he should give a call to one of his contacts in the British Secret Service, see if he could get a line on a military transport. *Some* pilot could fly in this weather. This was a life-or-death situation. He had no time for canned music, recycled coffee, and the condescending, lipsticked smiles of British Airways staff members. He glanced at the phones again. He hesitated, then shook his head. *No.* Calling the British Secret Service would take a while; even with Loki as a potential prize, nobody would authorize use of a military aircraft just so Tom could hurry to the States.

"Please have a seat, sir," the woman encouraged. "We're trying our very best."

"I know, I know," he muttered impatiently. He didn't mean to take out his frustration on this poor woman, but he was beyond putting a lid on his emotions. Loki had outplayed him, outsmarted him, and outstrategized him. And the one chance he had to level the playing field had been thwarted by *rain*. Rain!

Tom knew then why he was so enraged. It was the

lack of control. The feeling of powerlessness. The need for control was an addiction both he and his twin shared. It was what bound their lives together.

"This storm looks pretty bad," the woman murmured, breaking into Tom's thoughts. "The bottom line is that we don't risk lives. I can't say when you'll get out of here, sir, but you will. Not in the next three hours, but sometime thereafter. If you're lucky, you'll leave tonight. But it could be tomorrow."

"I. . . see." Tom nodded. At this point all he could do was pray. Too bad he wasn't a religious man. Not many obsessive control freaks were.

LOKI SMILED AS THE BLACK MERCEDES

limo glided to a stop in front of him. He opened the back door, gesturing to his bodyguard to sit up front. The man complied, rolling his massive bulk into the front passenger seat. A strong man, Viggo. Not intellectually overburdened, but his intellect wasn't what Loki needed tonight.

"Did you replenish the minibar?" he asked the

chauffeur as his eyes settled on the wood-paneled compartment running perpendicular to the plush leather seats in back.

The driver said nothing but pressed a button, and the compartment slid open. Oliver's smile widened. A full arsenal of weapons—knives, grenades, a machine gun, automatic and semiautomatic pistols—gleamed back at him from the storage space.

"Well done," he pronounced, caressing a medium-sized but exceptionally light 9mm Glock. It felt smooth to the touch. He gingerly removed it from its holster and tucked it into his breast pocket. The compartment door slid shut. "One can never be too careful. Now where to?"

"Tribeca, sir," Josh Kendall answered as he maneuvered the car onto Ninth Avenue. "Traffic's light. We'll be right on time."

GAIA RARELY VENTURED INTO TRIBECA.

A Bitch

But as she emerged from the Franklin Street subway stop—which, for some reason, was much cleaner and better kept than almost any subway stop she'd ever seen—she came to an abrupt, impulsive decision. *This* neighborhood was going to be her new hangout. Yeah, it was a perfect change from the mishmash of sleaze and chess freaks and college kids that was Washington Square Park. Unlittered streets. Expensive lofts. No traffic. Hardly a soul in sight, except a few rich young yuppies walking their dogs.

Hey, maybe she could even walk dogs for some extra cash. Maybe she could do it for a living. Why not? Dog walking was a pretty common job in New York City, second probably only to waitressing and drug dealing. What a life: Live uptown in a fabulous West Side apartment and commute to another fabulous neighborhood to hang out with canines. That was perfection. That was bliss.

She smiled as she strolled around the corner onto West Broadway. She wouldn't have believed it possible, but she actually felt halfway decent. Her life was changing—and in many ways, for the better. Sam was a part of some other era. Maybe there was a place for him in this new phase, but in some different role, some newfound incarnation. One that was a lot less complicated and painful.

The Bubble Lounge shed a reddish glow onto the street. Gaia could see dark shapes moving inside. She heard laughter. Always a good sign. *Relax,* she ordered herself, pushing through the heavy door into the restaurant. Mrs. Moss's words drifted through her mind: " . . . *remember, if you stick with something long enough, the bumps smooth themselves out in the end."* Right. Smooth like butter. But as she scanned the room for Sam, looking for those familiar tufts of light brown hair among the slick, gelled crew cuts and George-Clooney-style Caesars, her heart began pumping a hip-hop rhythm against her rib cage. Saying good-bye was a bitch. No matter how you sliced it. She knew that better than anyone—

There he is.

He was sitting on a couch at the back of the restaurant, absently sipping a soda. His eyes were dark and sad and brooding—and the sight of them instantly transported her back to that first rainy day in the park, when so much had passed between them in silence. She swallowed, feeling the room swirl around her and recede into nothingness. Everything had been encapsulated in that first chess game; it set the tone for their entire relationship. They'd tortured themselves by playing in the rain, not wanting to leave, not wanting to sever the cord of tension and attraction. And they'd carried that pattern of masochism all through their relationship until the cord had inevitably snapped.

It went wrong because it could never go right.

He waved, tentatively, his jacket sleeve falling loosely about his wrist.

She nodded.

And as she had in the park that first day, she felt a

nameless urge to turn and bolt. The lyrics of a new Fearless song pulsed through the restaurant and seemed to vibrate through Gaia's body: *"Still bending my mind, warping my will / you hypnotize with your lying eyes. . . ."*

Sam let his hand drop in slow motion, a frame or two behind real time.

But maybe there was some tension left in the cord after all. She didn't need to get ahead of herself. Why plan for the future? Planning had never gotten her very far. Maybe tonight wasn't about official good-byes. Maybe it about her and Sam simply being together. Playing it by ear. Talking and listening. Maybe tonight was just dinner. She was hungry, after all. She could use a little sustenance.

Of all the bizarre
scenarios she'd
envisioned for
this evening—a

invisible

screaming fight, a
tearful **sniper**

embrace, a
passionate kiss—
she would never have
conceived of *this*.

FINALLY.

Tom expelled a heavy sigh as the Concorde slowly rolled back from the gate. He'd gotten a lucky break. Maybe the British Airways staff didn't want to hear any more complaining; maybe there had just been some unforeseen change in the weather, a brief window of opportu-  nity. Whatever the reason, the passengers had suddenly been rushed onto the plane only an hour later than the original scheduled departure.

It was still pouring, harder than before. Rain pounded the fuselage. Tom peered out the window, seeing only his reflection in the blackness.

"Champagne?"

A pretty young flight attendant was hovering over him, her blue eyes twinkling as she held out a tray of champagne flutes.

Tom shook his head. Alcohol was the last thing he needed. He glanced down at his watch. 2:00 A.M. Greenwich mean time. 9:00 P.M. eastern standard time. . . His mind began calculating possibilities. He could be on the streets of New York by midnight. That was the beauty of the Concorde; one could take off later than one landed—by traveling west, across time zones in reverse. And even if the fact of "going back in time" was merely psychological, Tom welcomed the phony edge it gave him. A phony edge was better than no edge at all.

His fingers drummed the briefcase on his lap. Inside was the disk—the disk that held a secret so vile that nobody could possibly believe it. No, CLOFAZE had to be experienced firsthand, and even then it tested the limits of plausibility. That was why Tom had yet to alert George or anyone else at the Agency as to its existence. If he tried explaining it over the phone, they would simply think he'd cracked. His behavior had been erratic enough over the past few months. They'd send somebody out to rein him in or terminate him—most likely the latter.

"Good evening, passengers," an amiable British voice announced over the plane's speaker system.

Tom tuned out the pilot as he introduced himself on the intercom, apologizing for the delay. *Refocus.* It was hard to concentrate when he was in such a passive position, at the mercy of pilots and the weather control. But as the Concorde's powerful engines rumbled to life, he tried to exorcise the doubt gnawing away at his insides. Briefly it worked, until the Concorde turned onto the runway and paused. With a mighty roar the plane began to gather speed—faster and faster.

This plane was a lot like his twin.

Loki was fast, too. And powerful. And seductive.

And he was in the same city as Gaia.

Tom gripped the armrests of his chair. He couldn't give in to desperation. He couldn't give in to the big black hole of negative thinking. He breathed deeply, evenly, consciously—employing a style of meditation he'd taught Gaia long ago, when he'd first started training her in kung fu. And as he breathed, Tom concentrated all of his energies into a silent speech to his daughter: *Don't allow yourself to be deceived. Stay strong.*

SAM STARED AT THE MEAL IN FRONT

of him: medium-rare steak with sweet potato fries and creamed spinach. It turned his stomach. There was no way he could eat. But he had to look at the food. It was either that or look at Gaia.

Slippery Fish

How could he even *sit* here—across from her, perpetrating this fraud? He'd seen the emotional exhaustion in her clear blue eyes. It was like looking into a mirror. He couldn't even define his feelings anymore. His thoughts were slippery fish; if he tried to grab one, it would wriggle from his grasp. *Oliver. Gaia. Josh. Tom.* Maybe, despite his sick methods, Oliver really *did* have Gaia's best interests at heart. Oliver certainly seemed to be a lot more focused on Gaia than her father. Sam swallowed, feeling eyes on him—eyes that might or might not even have existed. A high-power rifle could be aimed at his head right now. Even here. Even in the calm of this restaurant. A hidden microphone could be listening to every word.

He pushed a piece of meat around his plate with his fork. He was a prisoner. And there was only one way to escape.

"So." Gaia put down her fork. It clanged loudly on the plate, a not-so-subtle signal that she was tired of silence. Sam was forced to lift his gaze. "You said you wanted to talk. Let's talk."

"Do you mind if we wait a little?" Sam murmured. He stared at a spot just below her lips. His head had begun to throb. He touched the side of his temple gingerly.

"Are you okay?" Gaia asked. Her face creased in concern. "I mean, are you sick or something? You haven't touched your food."

Sam nodded. "Yeah. I mean, no." He tried to smile. He imagined himself smashing his plate into small pieces. The way he'd smashed his own heart. "I'm okay," he whispered hoarsely, suddenly reaching out and grabbing Gaia's hand. He'd done it without thinking. A drowning man, desperate for a life preserver. He stared at her flesh, soaking in every beautiful feature: the slender bones, the soft skin, the fingers graceful and long, the power that lay beneath them.

"I don't think. . . ." Gaia didn't finish. Instead she simply withdrew her hand and resumed eating. "I—I'm sorry."

Blackness ate at the edges of his vision. That one little gesture told Sam everything he needed to know. He'd lost her. *No!* He wouldn't accept that. He lifted his gaze and saw that her face was flushed. She ate quickly, probably filling her mouth so that she wouldn't have to speak.

"I'm sorry." Sam groped for words, his eyes skittering nervously around the room, wondering again if Oliver was listening or watching. "I guess it's just a force of habit. When we're here like this together, I still. . . I still feel close to you."

Gaia nodded. Her face betrayed no emotion. She chewed loudly. But she was blinking, very rapidly. Hope flickered inside him. She was wrestling with pain and uncertainty and longing, too—and trying not to show it. The chess game had resumed. He still had a chance.

"There's something else," Sam whispered.

She swallowed. "What's that?"

"I've spoken with your uncle."

Her fork fell to the plate again. She looked like she'd been slapped. Her eyes flashed with disbelief. "You *what?*" she hissed. "When did—"

"He stopped by my dorm the other night," Sam lied.

"Why?" she spat.

"He. . . he was reluctant to go see you himself. I mean, so soon after he'd asked you to come live with him." Sam wanted to close his eyes and staple his own mouth shut. He wanted that invisible sniper to pull the trigger. But he simply repeated the words he'd rehearsed for Josh and the thug. His body had become a cassette player, a machine, an instrument to convey words that weren't his. "I guess he figured that I would have a pretty good idea of the way you felt about things. I, uh, well—he didn't exactly know that we'd broken up or anything. He just. . . he just wanted to get to know me. To get to know about your life, without having to bother you."

Gaia didn't say a word. She didn't move. There was a glint of something behind her eyes, but Sam couldn't pinpoint it. Finally she took a deep breath.

"What did he want, Sam?" she asked. "I mean, really. What did he *want?*"

Sam met her gaze. His soul was a cave—hollow, dark, and cold. "He didn't want anything," he said. "Not from me, anyway. What he wants is for you to live with him. Starting now."

GAIA'S SHOULDERS TENSED. SHE

sat rigid as a nail. Of all the bizarre scenarios she'd envisioned for this evening—a screaming fight, a tearful embrace, a passionate kiss—she would never have conceived of *this*.

She didn't know whether to feel revulsion over the fact that Oliver had been sneaky and underhanded enough to try to get Sam on his side or excitement for the exact same reason. Maybe Oliver really *had* gone to Sam because he wanted to keep his word about giving her time. Maybe his surprise visit to Sam had been about respecting her wishes. About respecting *her,* period.

But then why did Sam look so shifty and uncertain? If she didn't know any better, she'd say that he was terrified. His skin was bloodless and pale, and his hands shook like leaves in his lap. But what could he possibly have to fear—*here,* of all places?

"Sam?" Gaia prompted softly. "Are you—?"

"Let me finish." He jerked suddenly, as if he'd fallen asleep and suddenly remembered where he was. His hands stopped shaking. He stared intensely into Gaia's face. The look there was blank. Sam Moon was no longer present. At least not in any real sense. If the eyes were truly the windows of the soul, then Sam had just drawn the shades. He'd slipped back into actor mode.

"Your uncle really loves you, Gaia," Sam said. "And from what I could tell, it would be great for you to be with family again."

Gaia's face shriveled in bewilderment. The words were stilted, tinny—totally unlike Sam. He sounded like he was reading from a poorly written script. He wasn't just lying; he was reciting something he'd obviously prepared. But why? What purpose did this serve? Maybe he really *had* gone insane. Or maybe this was a sick way of ending their relationship forever. A way of ensuring that they would never have to see each other again. After all, if she went with Oliver, she'd be leaving the country. Perhaps for a few months. Perhaps forever.

"He's got all sorts of plans—"

"Sam!" Gaia interrupted hoarsely. Anger began to take hold. "Stop it, all right? Tell me what the hell is going on. Really. Say what's on your mind. For once."

He blinked. "I am, Gaia," he continued, his voice still as neutral and toneless as a talking toy's. "It's important that you get the love you've missed out on all these years. Your uncle seems to be the man for the job. Don't you think so, Gaia?"

The love I've missed out on. . . the man for the job. . . .

An electric fizz began to hum inside her veins. The anger receded, replaced with a cool alertness. The words of a talking toy. Yes, that's precisely what they were. The words of a puppet. This was a puppet show. Sam *was* reading a script. One that had been prepared *for* him. The phrases he used, his mannerisms—they were totally alien. Somebody was forcing him to do this—

"Don't you think so, Gaia?" Sam repeated.

His voice had shifted again. Gone was the

neutrality. The tone was almost threatening. Gaia stared at him. Her pulse quickened.

And that's when she saw the shades part behind his
eyes. Only for a split second. Barely time for anything
to register. But it was enough. She caught a glimpse of
something there. A silent message.

I'm afraid. Help me.

"You should have heard the things Oliver told me,"
Sam went on. "He's traveled all around the world, but
he never. . . ."

Gaia was no longer listening to his words. She for-
got her confusion, the purpose of the evening, the
restaurant—all of it. He was trying to tell her something. *What?* She focused all of her energy on trying to
decipher the secret of Sam's eyes, which pleaded with
her to understand that something was wrong.

And that's when it hit her.

They were in danger.

LOKI RAISED THE INFRARED BINOC-
ulars to his eyes and nodded in satisfaction. There
they were: two silhouettes
outlined against the cur-
tain of the Bubble Lounge.

Sleek Black Shark

They were leaning close together. A sign of intimacy. A part of him seethed with rage, but he shut it off, as if it were a noisy appliance. Intimacy was required. Gaia trusted this boy. And in turn, that trust would be siphoned to Loki himself. One couldn't dispose of emotion. One could only redirect it. He knew that from experience. He knew that from watching, as if from a distance, his love of Katia shift to this wondrous girl—this daughter he should have had.

"Is the other car in position?" he asked.

"Yes, sir," Josh replied, slowing.

"Maintain your speed," Loki barked.

The Mercedes limo lurched forward again—a sleek black shark, rounding the block and returning slowly to circle once again. They needed to park soon. Loki didn't want to attract any undue attention to himself. But he did want to watch. . . .

"Has our little undergrad learned his script well?" Loki asked Josh.

"Very," Josh replied. "He knows what's good for him. And he loves her. Everything has gone the way you said it would. I think he really believes that her moving in with you is the best thing for her."

Loki's lips flattened. He sat back, reclining deep into the leather seat. "Of course he does," Loki breathed. "Because it's true."

". . . WHAT IT COMES DOWN TO,

in the end, is that he wants to take care of you," Sam finished. "He wants to provide for you."

Spelling It Out

Gaia didn't seem to hear him. Which was good. Because his eyes screamed in contradiction to his words. At least he prayed they did. They held horror; they held warnings; they never moved. And she was starting to understand. He could see that. The time was coming to make his move.

"I see," she said blankly, after a few seconds of silence.

A cloud of confusion flitted across her face. He shook his head, unable to control himself. Did she doubt him? Did she doubt his fear? Had he been lying for so long to her that she could no longer tell the difference between reality and the shield that protected it? No, he couldn't let her take that route. He had to reach her. He wanted to shout at her. But couldn't risk it. Oliver was listening; Oliver would end this conversation in the blink of an eye. *Oh God.* His breathing was shallow. He was starting to panic. Deep breaths. He wasn't dead yet. He was still on the board. That was his mantra, his salvation. *Still on the board.*

"Sounds like you had quite a conversation," Gaia added.

"Yeah." Sam nodded. He twisted and glanced over his shoulder. His thighs were so sticky with sweat that they were practically glued to his seat. Nobody around him seemed suspicious-looking; in fact, no new customers had entered the restaurant. But that didn't mean a damn thing. The gun sight could still be aimed at his head. It *was* aimed at his head.

Still, they couldn't see inside him. Or inside her. No one could eavesdrop on their silence, their private language. Sam just had to keep sending the message, boring his eyes into hers, beaming the truth from that part of him that Gaia still trusted: the Sam that would never lie. His hands trembled again. Their gazes had locked, suspended in a moment of total synchronicity. He had to hold on to it, to keep her there, to—

And then he saw it. A needle flash of red light. Behind the curtain, from the street.

Or had he just imagined it?

"Sam?" Gaia whispered.

That was all it took. He surrendered to panic. He wasn't strong enough for this.

"Gaia," he whispered. He reached out and grasped her wrists so tightly, she flinched. "You have to get out of here. Right now."

No response. Nothing. The connection had been severed. His grip tightened on her flesh, digging into her bones. The seconds stretched into aeons.

His stomach somersaulted as he glimpsed the shadows of two dark, massive cars slowing to a stop on the street outside. *Shit.* The second car was right out front. His eyes narrowed. It was close—close enough for Sam to make out the person at the wheel. Josh. Even behind the veil of the curtain, Sam would recognize that face anywhere.

Gaia shook her head. "Sam, I need you to—"

"Listen to me." Sam loosened his grip on Gaia's wrists, willing himself to stay seated, willing Gaia back to that plateau of synchronicity. "I want you to stand up and walk away, like you're going to the rest room. Go out the back. Do it."

Hesitation registered in Gaia's face, in the tiny ripple on her forehead.

Sam heard a door slam outside. He turned.

Josh was out of the car.

Sam sprang to his feet, grabbed Gaia's hand, and pulled her away from the table. The waiting was over. It was time to run.

IT WAS LIKE BEING CAUGHT IN A dream—the kind of dream where nothing makes sense, where the rational laws that govern the universe cease to

Seething Jumble

exist but you go through the motions of absurdity, anyway. Gaia surrendered to it. She allowed herself to be pulled by Sam—through a gaggle of yuppies near the bar, through some tables, then downstairs to the rest rooms. Her feet flopped awkwardly on the steps. The adrenaline was still coursing through her veins, but her mind was a brick wall. Nothing could get in. Or out. "Shouldn't have waited," Sam mumbled breathlessly.

But whether he was addressing her or himself, she had no clue.

She stole a glance over her shoulder. At the top of the staircase was a bald man in a dark suit. And... was that Josh? Yeah. It was. Sam's weird RA. Her eyes narrowed. He and the bald guy were looking around upstairs, as if they couldn't decide whether or not to come down to the basement. What was Josh doing here? Was this just a coincidence? Why did he—

"Come on," Sam grunted, yanking her through a set of swinging double doors into the kitchen—past a bemused busboy, a sizzling stove, two surly-looking chefs. Sam's hand was hot, damp. She clenched it in her own, matching his pace. There were flashes of aluminum, countertops, industrial refrigerators—and finally an exit.

Wordlessly they broke apart and began to run. Their feet slapped the pavement in unison as they hurtled down an alleyway, past the restaurant garbage cans, toward an avenue. Gaia's head was spinning like a top. She didn't question the motivation behind this crazed sprit. She'd seen the fear on Sam's face. Words from the past surged through her memory, snatches of conversation with Sam. In the park. On the phone. *I can't tell you what's going on. . . . It's not what you think. . . . Trust me, Gaia. . . .* The words collided with images. The hunted look in his eyes. Josh's mysterious appearance in Chinatown. The way Sam had pushed Gaia away from Josh. The hatred in his glare.

The questions thudded louder than her heartbeat. Her thoughts were a seething jumble of mismatched pictures and Sam's stilted excuses.

What was the connection?

Gaia's lungs were burning by the time they reached end of the alley. She scanned the avenue, the cars and cabs whizzing past them.

"You've got to get away," Sam told her, his voice broken and ragged as he struggled for breath. His body was bent, hands on his knees to steady himself.

"Tell me what's going on, Sam," Gaia begged. "What does Josh—"

"Later." He shook his head, cutting her off. Drops of sweat fell from his hair. His eyes were wide and skittish. "They'll find us soon enough. He's got men."

"Who does? Josh? Sam, you have to tell me what's

going on. I can't do this anymore. Give me some answers."

"I will." Sam steadied himself by placing his hands on Gaia's shoulders. "But first I have to distract them. You have to get away from me, Gaia. They want *you*. You're the one in danger."

Gaia's chest felt tight as a drum. Sam's voice was filled with desperation, knowledge, terror. Something had happened to him, something profound. It had changed him. It lay at the root of everything that had happened. She didn't need to understand fear to feel it in Sam. "I'm not leaving you," she heard herself say. "No way I leave without you." Her voice broke on the last word. Tears clawed at her eyelids. Her mind still ran in loops, an endless fast-forward and rewind, scanning for answers. But her heart was in the here and now. With Sam. She was going nowhere without him. "Why don't we just—"

"*No!*" he shouted. He backed away from her. "I'll find you. You have to do what I say. It's the only way. You have to trust me now. You haven't trusted me in a very long time. But trust me now."

Trust me now. There they were. Those words again. Regret and confusion mingled with her tears. Why had she ever stopped trusting Sam? He loved her. She loved him—

Sam lunged forward and crushed her lips with his own.

Gaia reciprocated. Nothing made sense— nothing but this: the most basic, physical, visceral connection. She felt like she'd swallowed an exploding star. Her arms tightened around his waist, her eyes closed, and then they were spinning together. Alone in the dark, just the two of them. This was all they'd ever needed to do. Ever. When they'd started spiraling away from each other. When the wobbly moments had tortured them. *We should have just kissed.* In their kisses there were no questions, no doubts, no distance. There was nothing except love.

And then he pulled away from her.

He sprinted down Hudson Street and vanished around a corner.

He was gone.

Gaia paused in the darkness. *Sam.* His name caught in her throat. She wanted to shout it, to ask him to turn around because suddenly seeing his face again seemed vitally important. But she didn't. She stumbled in the opposite direction. She had to be strong. She had to listen to Sam, to vanish into the night before they found her. Whoever "they" were. Sam knew what was happening. Sam had the answers.

Sam will find me, Gaia told herself as she hurried down the avenue. *We'll find each other. We always do.*

Then came
the pain. It
suffused
every
crevice of
his being,
replacing
strength
with
weakness.

**two
dead
stones**

SAM HELD HIS BREATH, PEERING
out from behind a brick wall
until Gaia was gone from
sight. Then he exhaled. The
game of cat and mouse was
over. Finally over. He
felt an odd sense of relief. It
was time to end the chase.

Still on the Board

But the relief quickly faded as he circled back
toward the alley behind the Bubble Lounge. His
feet were like stone. Every part of his body fought
to resist, to chase after Gaia, to grab her hand and
run until they couldn't breathe anymore. It was
pure, animal instinct: moving toward the
enemy was wrong. Sam's intellect was stronger
than his instinct, though. Oliver and Josh would
get Gaia if he didn't put himself in their way. He
would stall them long enough for her to make an
escape.

You're still on the board, he said to himself. *You're
still on the board.*

He rounded the corner.

Four shadowy figures loomed in the darkness by
the kitchen door.

Sam swallowed, marching purposefully toward
them. One of them stepped forward. In the uncertain
half-light Sam saw that it was Josh. There was a flash
of silver in his hand.

"What do you think you're doing, Moon?" he demanded.

Sam throat tightened. His eyes fell to the gun. The other figures emerged. One was the stocky man who had showed up at his suite with Josh; another was the burly guy who'd brought Sam his food in Oliver's loft. Their faces blended together, indistinguishable. And finally there was Oliver himself, his eyes glittering like blue diamonds in the dark.

"Yes," Oliver whispered. "Do tell."

Calm. Stay calm. The muscles in Sam's neck tensed. Time to put on the show of his life. To lie like he'd never lied, to act like he'd never acted. Gaia would be inspiration. He pictured her running through the streets, full of questions, full of doubts about her family, her boyfriend, the fragile world she'd worked so hard to keep from falling apart.

"Nothing," Sam said. "I was sitting there having dinner, and she got up and bolted. I chased after her, but she disappeared."

Oliver exchanged a quick glance with the three others. "Funny," he said. "From our angle it looked like you were pulling her out of the restaurant."

Sam shrugged. He stared Josh in the eye with as much defensive calm as he could muster and for the first time saw him for who he truly was. Josh was nothing more than a puppet himself. A guy who'd played a role for too long. Many roles. In the shadow of Oliver he was the dutiful servant. In Sam's presence he was the menacing false buddy. And who was he really? He probably didn't know himself. After all, he'd been operating in this world for much longer than Sam, and Sam could barely remember *his* real identity.

"Did you say something to her?" Josh asked. He raised the pistol slightly.

Again Sam shrugged. A hot smog filled his chest, clogging his lungs, threatening to suffocate him.

"There's a question pending," Oliver stated.

"We were having dinner," Sam said. His throat was very dry. "I was telling her how much you wanted her back, and she just got up and bolted."

Oliver smiled. It was by far the most disturbing smile Sam had ever seen because there was absolutely no warmth behind it. His bird eyes were two dead stones.

"You're lying again, Sam," he said.

"No, I'm not." Sam's toes were curling in his shoes. His lashes fluttered rapidly. His knees had begun to tremble. The signs were all there: his body was reacting to the danger, irrespective of his mind. A jolt of adrenaline rattled his nerves. He wouldn't be able to keep still much longer.

"You're telling me that Gaia ran away," Oliver said.

It wasn't a question. It was a statement. Sam's heart

began to slam into his rib cage then. Panic was speeding toward him like a train. *Steady.*

"Gaia—she, well, she doesn't trust me," he stammered. "She smelled a rat as soon as I mentioned your name. She didn't believe any of it. I tried to make her listen, but she got up and ran. I managed to follow her for a while, but you know Gaia. . . ." His voice faded. He didn't have the breath to continue. His lungs were working too hard.

"Yes," Oliver said. "I do know Gaia. And I know what's best for her." He looked Sam in the eye. "I'll ask you this once. Where did she go?"

Sam shook his head. "I—uh, she didn't say." Unconsciously he took a step back. His joints and limbs were singing now, screaming in unison for him to turn and run.

Oliver nodded. "Very well," he said. His gaze briefly flashed to Josh. Then he turned and disappeared back into the kitchen. The other two thugs followed him. Only Josh remained. The hairs on the back of Sam's neck rose. The silence stretched between them. Sam took another step back.

"Well, Sammy, bro, it was nice working with you," Josh said.

That was all Sam needed. Without a second thought he whirled and sprinted toward the back of the alley. Something occurred to him then, too: in some ways he'd never felt more alive than he did at this moment.

Fear, triumph, terror, love—a maelstrom of a thousand competing emotions rocked his brain as his body pushed itself to the limit, every muscle aching, every bone pounding.

You helped Gaia, Sam told himself as his breathing deepened, his lungs straining for more oxygen. And nobody could ever take that away from him. Maybe Oliver or Sam would catch up to her sooner or later— but for now, for the present, she was safe. He'd achieved his mission. He'd salvaged something precious from a life that had become worthless: his own.

That was when he heard it.

It was nothing more than a light ping—almost lost in the sound of his scrambling, burning feet. At the same time something struck his back. A punch. Josh must have chased him and punched him. Only it burned.

Sam didn't fall, but he did stumble forward a couple of steps. He couldn't keep running. That punch had sucked the energy out of him. Reflexively his hand darted behind his back. There was wetness on his fingers.

Then came the pain. It suffused every crevice of his being, replacing strength with weakness. He was confused suddenly. Disoriented. Time expanded like a loaf of bread in an oven, every moment stretching and stretching.

He glanced down at his shirt.

There was a dark splotch about the size and shape of a saucer, right next to his belly button. And there was a black hole in the center of it. He didn't understand what was happening. He staggered, righted himself. The pain was bad, but he could go on. Was that Gaia on the avenue, waiting at the end of the alley? He couldn't tell. And then suddenly he saw something else: the big house in Maryland, the front lawn buried in fall leaves.

Where's Sam? I can't see him!

His mother. Laughter. Then a different laugh. Lighter. Gaia's laugh, spinning around a chessboard, a giant chessboard, as big as his house—the fall leaves above her head in the park, dropping onto the black and white squares. And sound. Wind? Yes, a whistling wind... only it was getting weaker and weaker.

No. Keep breathing.

He was aware that he had dropped to his knees, but he could no longer fight the tide that was dragging him out to sea, pulling him under the surface. The world around him began to dim. It shrank until it was gone. Only sound remained: the sound of his own lungs, the strain of his breath, the whoosh of the exhale.

Gaia's face floated before him, a disembodied testament to beauty.

Sam smiled a crooked smile. *Wait for me!* But she

never did. She always had been so hard to keep. Didn't matter. He would get to her. Somehow he would get to her. He was nearly there. He felt another punch through the middle of his back—although oddly enough, there was no pain. Only pressure. And blackness. Disconnected fragments: *Sorry, Heather, I didn't get a chance to phone you back. . . . Mike, don't forget to meet me in the library. Where is my prescription? What time is it? How many heartbeats per minute? Cause of death? Gaia, wait up, I'm nearly there. I'm still on the board. . . .*

The last thought faded from his skull, and with it, the last frayed remnant of his life.

GAIA LEAPED INTO A DESERTED

car of the uptown A express train the instant before the subway doors closed. Trembling, she gulped for air. The train pulled away from the station. She fell into a plastic seat, exhausted. Where was she going? Definitely not back to the Mosses. No way. She might

Train Smash

have been followed, and she would never put them in danger. She probably *had* been followed. She needed to keep running, then rest; she needed to piece it all together. To plan ahead. But she couldn't think. Not now. Her body was too low on energy, her mind too filled with worry for Sam.

The train rattled into the darkness of a tunnel.

Gaia put her head in her hands. She felt sick for him, for what he'd gone through on her behalf. Because now it was all clear—if not in detail, then at least in shape. All the mystery, all the unexplained disappearances and strange behavior: Sam was being used. Someone had threatened him. To get to her.

But who? Oliver? Was *that* why he'd come to see Sam?

No. That was impossible. If Oliver wanted to see her, all he had to do was come knocking on her door. This had something to do with Sam's suite mate. Maybe with the kid who had died, too. Mike Suarez. At least, that would be the most likely scenario. . . .

Gaia's eyelids flickered as the stations flew past her. If she had learned anything from this madness, it was that anything could happen. No scenario was more likely than the next. The holes in the quilt were bigger than the quilt itself. But there was one crucial piece of information Gaia had gleaned from tonight's nightmare: Sam had kept secrets from her not because he was trying to shut her out of his life, but because he was trying to protect her.

That was all that mattered. Far more than the harsh words she'd said to him. Far more than the anger, the denial. He knew that. Besides, regret wasn't of any use to anyone, least of all Sam and her. And experiencing it here in the subway tunnel somehow felt even more pathetically useless. She sniffed, forced back her tears. Sam would be fine. They would be fine. And one day they'd look back on this as a terribly dramatic hiccup. A setback. A bump in the road. But not a train smash. Nothing like that.

She sighed and leaned back in her seat, then closed her eyes.

Maybe if I wait for him at his dorm. . . .

Her ears pricked up at the sound of the door at the end of the car swinging open. A blast of rushing subway wheels sliced through the silence of the empty car.

The door swung shut.

Footsteps approached. Two pairs. They stopped directly in front of her.

Gaia's eyelids opened. She found herself staring into a couple of familiar yet oddly unremarkable faces: the men who had attacked her in the park in January. Instantly her muscles tensed. Her nerves sprang to life. The jolt of energy was like an injection, hot and sickeningly sweet. But her face remained as blank as the two that stared back at her. As always, her mind drained of thought. Only five silent words remained.

I will never be free.

The men were carrying pistols. Their arms hung at

their sides; the silencers poked from the sleeves of their leather jackets.

"You'll be getting off with us at the next station," the one on the right stated. His tone wasn't threatening. In fact, it was almost polite.

The train began to slow.

The words melted away until no thoughts remained at all. `There was only formless rage.` Gaia lashed out with her left foot, surprising herself with the force of the kick. Her toe connected with the left man's groin: *smack!* He doubled over, cringing. With her left hand she snatched the pistol from his grasp by the silencer—simultaneously exploding out of her seat. Her right knee caught the man on the right in the solar plexus, and she whirled around, smashing the butt of the gun over his head.

He collapsed to the floor.

The train brakes screeched. Gaia stumbled backward. *Balance!* she furiously commanded herself.

The man on the left clutched at his groin, but he was still standing. Gaia shifted the gun to her right hand and cracked the bloodied gun butt against his left temple. His knees wobbled, but he didn't go down. As she staggered slightly, her eyes flashed to the first man. He was struggling to aim his gun at her. His eyes were unsteady. She didn't hesitate. She aimed at his left kneecap and fired. The sound of impact was much louder than the soft *thwip* of the shot. `A froth of` blood and bone shrapnel exploded from the joint—and the man shrieked. Amazingly, though, he didn't drop the gun.

Gaia turned her attention to the man on the left just as the train lurched to a halt. Their eyes met. She raised the gun, again aiming for the kneecap. But before she could pull the trigger, the man whirled and bolted for the doors—leaping off the train the moment they slid open, one hand still cupped over his crotch. He vanished into the station.

Luckily the platform was deserted. Gaia couldn't afford to be spotted standing over a man she had just shot. But nobody boarded her car. For a second there was a perfect silence. It was shattered by the piercing two-tone chime that signaled departure. The doors slid shut just as Gaia took aim at the man one more time—this time at his forehead.

"Who do you work for?" she hissed. Her heart pounded. She felt dizzy. She knew she was going to pass out soon. It was only a matter of time.

The man didn't answer. His own gun was pointed straight at her heart.

"Answer me!" she shouted.

He blinked. His gun wavered.

Without warning, he shoved the barrel against his temple and fired.

"No!" Gaia shouted.

Too late. His head fell back against the floor,

his eyes staring vacantly at the ceiling, the same blank expression on his lifeless face. Blood seeped from a small, neat round hole in his head. Gaia swallowed. The train sped into darkness. This man would rather die than answer her question. Which meant only one thing, of course: he feared his employer more than he feared death.

Using the hem of her dress, Gaia furiously wiped her own gun clean, then dropped it on top of his body. Then she turned and ran. She ran from car to car, never once stopping or looking back. She ran until the train reached the next station, then jumped off and transferred to another line. She didn't even know which line it was. Nor did she particularly care. Because by that point, the weakness and exhaustion she'd manage to ignore for those final seconds had grown into a mammoth cloud that enveloped her completely, shutting out everything else in the world.

Disappeared

NEITHER GEORGE NOR TOM HAD SPOKEN

a word since George had met Tom at the British Airways passenger terminal at JFK, then sped off into the night. There was nothing to say. The two of them sat in silence as George pulled his car onto the Brooklyn-Queens Expressway. Tom fidgeted, unable to keep still. Luckily his flight had landed a few minutes ahead of schedule. It wasn't even midnight—

Bee-bee-bee-beep.

George's cell phone. He reached into his windbreaker pocket, keeping one hand on the wheel, then flicked it open.

"Yes?" he said.

Tom stared at him.

George scowled. He flicked the phone shut and shoved it back into his pocket. "They lost her."

"What?" Tom cried. "How—"

"I don't know," George muttered. His eyes were very dark as he scanned the road. The Manhattan Bridge loomed ahead of them. "Her tail followed her from the Moss apartment. He caught the One train and saw her get off at Franklin. He followed her out of the subway car, but—"

"But what?" Tom demanded.

George shook his head in annoyed disbelief, the skin on his gaunt face seeming to tighten. "Once he got out into the street, he somehow managed to follow the wrong girl."

Tom couldn't even respond. He'd gone numb. Of all the incompetence, of all the stupidity. . . but no, he couldn't let anger affect him right now. He stared gloomily out at the city, shimmering across the East River. Arguably the greatest skyline in the world. A million pinpricks of light, mountains of concrete and glass all reaching up to the heavens in a great gesture of greed and ambition and hubris—a Tower of Babel. Yes, this skyline signified only doom right now. Because somewhere in that urban jungle was his daughter. This was a city that could swallow a person whole and never spit them out.

There was another ring. The car phone this time. George jabbed a button next to the gearshift.

"Yes?"

"They're canvassing the entire Tribeca area, sir," an unrecognizable voice announced over the speaker. "The Agency put an extra task force on it. She cannot have simply disappeared."

"I know," George stated. "I've already gotten that information—"

"There's something else, sir."

Tom swallowed. He turned to George. George's eyes remained fixed to the road.

"Yes?" George said.

"Sam Moon's body has been found. Two bullets in the back. An alleyway in Tribeca."

Tom's jaw dropped. He felt a prickling of dread in his stomach.

"How long?" George asked, his voice quavering.

"Body's still warm. Maybe two, three hours."

George gunned the engine. Tom knew that they didn't need to discuss this, either. The news spoke for itself: either Gaia had been captured or she'd managed to escape.

And either way, they'd lost her.

There's only one feeling worse than loneliness: guilt.

If you feel it strongly enough, it can smother you. And right now I'm having a hard time coming up for air. Because all I can think about is Sam. How I let my own blindness and self-involvement cloud my perception. My dad trained me pretty well, but not well enough. Otherwise I would have picked up something. I would have figured out that Sam was in deep trouble. That he was trying to save me. Protect me. And that he'd watched himself turn into a monster in the process.

It's my fault.

I wish he'd told me something. But he must have had a very good reason to keep silent. I still don't even know how it all happened. Or what happened. I have a few clues, a shitload of gaps, and a very strong feeling that I will find out the answers to all of this soon enough. They say

love means never having to say
you're sorry. That's a lie,
though. In my experience, love is
all about being sorry. And I'm
sorry, Sam. I loved you once. A
part of me still loves you now
and always will. I wish I could
tell you that face-to-face, but
it will have to wait until we see
each other again.

For now, I have to lie low.
And that means leaving everyone
and everything behind. No
friends, no loved ones, nothing.

Strange. It feels a little
like déjà vu.

F E A R L E S S

. . . a girl born without the fear gene

I thought I loved Sam.

He betrayed me.

Now he's gone.

I thought I loved my uncle.

He doesn't know what love is.

He only wants to use me.